THE
POWERFUL

CONNOR VALLEE

First Printing, 2020

ISBN 978-1-09831-008-0

Editor: Yael Katzwer
Cover and chapter art: Jasricart
Author photo: Kristen Pierce
Text formatting: Connor Vallee

Printed in the United States of America by BookBaby

To the people who never gave up on me.

&

To my Madison, you will be remembered always.

THE
POWERFUL

INTRODUCTION

This isn't a world someone would choose to live in and no one would ever choose this fate. But the truth is she has no choice. It's as if she were made to push against these forces that would push against her. Her strength prevails over any Power you could ever meet. Although her world could shatter at any moment, she holds the world up by fighting the very forces working to hold her back. But can she survive? This world is full of hate, greed, and people who strive to serve only one purpose—to kill.

Welcome to our world.

PROLOGUE

"So you expect me to just sit around and let us die?"

"Trevor, baby," my mom pleaded.

"Meanwhile he is laughing at both of us. I'm not backing down," my father yelled, his muscular shoulders tensed and fists clenched. His usually perfectly combed over hair a complete mess.

"You know it's useless to fight him. You know it."

"Well, we die and what happens to Annie? Hmm?"

At five years old these arguments were terrifying. Unfortunately, they were becoming more common every day. But what could I do?

"She will be okay. Trevor, look at me." He looked up and it was clear from the look in his eyes that he was drunk. "She will be okay. I will make sure of it, but please don't leave me, baby. Please," she begged, resting her hand gently on his shoulder.

He looked at my mother, a beautiful woman. She had long blonde hair and gorgeous sky-blue eyes, her facial features defined yet somehow gentle. Her fair skin, once aglow with life and power, was now dimmed with sickness. I watched my father's face relax as tears came to his eyes. Then he ran out the door.

I walked up to my mother and wrapped my arms around her legs. She wiped away a tear and picked me up. She held me so tightly and I burrowed my face into her long golden hair. Right then is when I knew things were not going to get better.

We spent the rest of the night watching movies on the couch and I felt my mom's eyes on me the entire time. She wanted to ease the mood, but I knew something was wrong.

"What's the matter, Mommy? Do you hate the movie?"

She stroked the side of my face, pushing my hair behind my ear. The corner of her mouth raised into a half smile. "No, baby. Of course not." She turned the TV off.

"You're scared about Daddy. Aren't you?"

"Yes. I am," she admitted.

"He's gonna be okay, mommy. He always comes home." I smiled at her. I had a general idea that the state of our family was bad, but I didn't understand why or what that meant for my future.

"Annie, honey, I am going to tell you some important things right now. Okay?" I nodded. "I have told you all about Powers and you know Mommy is one, right?" I nodded enthusiastically. "You are a very special girl and one day you will be as strong as Daddy and me, even stronger, but people are going to try to hurt you and keep you down for the very things that make you special. You have to stay strong, okay?" I nodded and wondered why she was telling me this. *Wasn't she always going to be there?* "You cannot let them win. Someday other people — just like you — will look up to your strength as a sort

4

of hope. You are an amazing person and you will only become better. Are you listening to me, sweetheart?"

"Yes, Mommy, I am, but where are you going?"

"I am always going to be with you." She reached behind her neck and unclasped her necklace, an unobtrusive purple amethyst dangling from a thick chain. As she held it in her hands, I watched the chain light up, the light traveling down to the stone. She put it around my neck and, as the light faded away, I felt a flow of warmth run through me, ending in my hands. "Keep me with you always, baby. Don't ever take your necklace off," she said, stroking my hair. "Do you trust me?"

"I do. I really do."

"Good, because ..."

The door slammed open with a shocking bang and there stood my dad. His clothes were torn and his skin was covered in large gashes—blood all over his hands.

"Lisa!" He was in far worse shape than he had been when he left. My mother pushed herself up, with much effort, and approached my father, who held a large serrated knife in his hand.

"Oh my God, Trevor, what happened?" my mother asked, horrified.

"He's coming for her! Right now! And I won't let that happen. I won't let him ruin her." Pushing my mom to the ground, he lunged at me and pushed me up against the wall.

"Daddy?!"

"I'm sorry, Annie, but you will be better off with us. Since we will be dead soon, it only makes sense if you are too." I felt a sharp pain in the middle of my chest from the knife my dad held against me, piercing my skin.

"Trevor! No! God no!" My mother's was voice taken over by desperation. "Trevor!" my mother desperately screamed once again.

He glanced at her as she lay sprawled on the floor, too weak to rise. Then he gazed at me, gently lowering me to the floor. He placed his big warm hands on either side of my face and stayed there watching me, studying me as if he would never see me again. I didn't move a muscle.

"I am so sorry, Annie." He kissed my forehead. "Please. Forgive me," he pleaded, having realized what he was really about to do to me.

As he walked back out the door, I crawled over to my mom. She fell back abruptly holding her hands to her head. She screamed out, "No, Josh!" We both crawled to the window, where we peered out and saw two dark figures standing with my father, and then they were gone in the blink of an eye.

I stayed by the window as my mom ran stumbling to the phone to call her brother, Brett. As usual, an argument began. She and her brother didn't have a great relationship. Every conversation incited an argument because, despite being raised in the same house, Brett had formed a corrosive hatred for Powers.

I overheard her mention Nick, the cousin I knew to be the closest in age to me. I had never met him though; my uncle went out of his way to avoid my family. My mom hung up the phone with a huge sigh and returned to me.

We lay down on the couch. I rested on her and she wrapped her arms around me.

"I love you more than anything in this world, Annie. I am sorry. Eternally sorry." I remained laying on her, my ear to her chest, her words vibrating through me. "You will understand what happened here when you are older. And I pray you will forgive me."

We stayed like this for a half an hour until we heard car doors slam. She lifted me off her and went to the door.

"Hey, Brett."

"Annalise." A blunt and unemotional greeting.

"I'm sorry about this." She walked him into my father's office, leaning on each surface to keep herself standing, and closed the door behind them. Nick walked up to me. He was eleven at the time.

"Hey, Annie," Nick said, smiling.

"Hi." I was so overwhelmed with everything, my mind spinning in a million different directions.

"I hear you are going to stay with us. That's cool!"

"What?" *What is he talking about?*

I think he kept talking, but I walked toward the office door. It seemed to loom before me. It held uncertainty behind it. I could hear their muffled voices. They were discussing money and support of some kind.

After what seemed like hours, they returned to the room Nick and I were in. My uncle was holding a thick stack of papers.

"We will be in the car. Come on, bud," he said to Nick.

My mother knelt in front of me, a sad smile on her face.

"Please, Mommy, don't go," I begged.

"You're a good girl, Annie." She pulled my head to her and kissed my forehead. I could feel a hot tear land on my face. When she pulled away she reached for my necklace and held the amethyst stone in her hand. "Keep me with you, always." I was crying more than I thought possible. She buckled me into the car and we drove away from her.

She was gone.

1
THE BASICS

I'm sorry for starting out with such a terrible memory, but to start anywhere else felt wrong. As you have probably realized, I am Annie. Annie James, but everyone in town knows me as Annie Winters, my uncle's last name and my mom's maiden name.

I'm sure you're wondering why I started with that story. I had to set the scene before I explained a few things. My parents were Powers and so am I. A Power is simply a person with supernatural abilities, but we aren't all the same. In addition to our DNA allowing us to be in perfect physical condition and have uncanny attractiveness, some of us are stronger than others and some of us have skills refined to specific abilities. Either way, we are different from the general population and, as history has shown again and again, the world doesn't really like *different*. That is where Hunters come in. Hunters: the people who dedicate their lives to killing Powers. But there is a catch; we can't just die. I am not saying bullets bounce off us or anything. No, no Superman status. A well placed shot to any major organ will knock us out for a few hours, sure, but it doesn't kill us. It *can't* kill us. Sounds fun, right?

Wrong.

Hunters capture and experiment on us, playing around with our DNA until they find our Formula. I should explain that, too. A Formula is Power specific. Each Power, like myself, has their own, because these Formulas target the exact parts of our DNA that make us, well, Powers. If the Formula is made correctly, it is the one thing that can kill us. It breaks down our DNA, strips away our powers, and makes us mere humans.

Oh just kidding. Not the only thing. Blood relatives can use their powers, very specifically, to kill each other. Why someone would want to kill their family member is beyond me, but unfortunately it is an option. I believe it has something to do with where our powers originate. I am not entirely sure; there is little research on the topic.

So why, you ask, are Hunters allowed to do this?

Well, let me take you back to 2033. Powers had just started coming out to the world, unafraid of adversity and hoping to live equally among humans. Some Powers didn't agree with putting us out in the open on a massive scale and, in return, a group formed. They called themselves the Triad. They had three secret locations around the globe and used them to plot an enormous attack on the human population. It was enormous alright. Over ten thousand humans were killed in 2036. It is safe to say that the Triad ruined it for the rest of us. Before this, Power hunting was a black-market service, more similar to hiring a mercenary than anything else. Well, after the Triad attack, humans passed legislation that stripped away our rights. For those who were clever enough and knew how to bend the law, find the most insidious loopholes, this legislation essentially made it legal to hunt and kill Powers. Anti-Power discrimination of all kinds became acceptable. Those in positions of authority turned a blind eye.

That is why I started with that story. My mom was dying because a Hunter had found her Formula, along with my father's. She was suffering because without her abilities, her body could not survive. Imagine if someone removed your heart and you kept living. How long could you last? I mean, sure, that sounds a bit extreme, but abilities are crucial to our very being and survival. We become incredibly sick without them.

Anyway, that is a general rundown of the life of a Power. Hopefully that helps you with understanding my story. In 2051 racism was at an all-time low; for the first time in a long time sexual identity and skin color were not really a concern among people. Mostly because people had another group to cast their hate upon. That, my friends, is where the Powers came in; we were the new outcasts.

2
FIRST DAY

When I was sixteen, I decided I was tired of waiting around in my jail cell of a room. I wanted to have at least *some* semblance of a normal teenage experience. An incident when I was ten had caused my uncle to lock me away; I wasn't about to go ask him for permission to return to school. So, I forged some documents, and told him when it was all said and done.

They were mainly the kind of documents stating I was a perfectly normal human girl getting a late start on her education. It took a little research, but the internet has all the necessary info to allow me to start high school.

It wouldn't be a problem. Catching up that is. During my years locked away I studied a range of different topics, basically homeschooling myself in all the necessary school subjects. Not to mention educating myself on everything I could find about Powers. I spent months researching the kind of Powers that existed and what Formulas normally consisted of.

I will admit, it was hard to find. Hunters tend to keep that information to themselves, to make them seem even more vital to the world's survival.

It's safe to say there wouldn't be much catching up necessary. Oh not to mention, my main ability is information retention. So I can remember things *stupid* fast.

Moving on.

❖ ❖ ❖

As I walked toward the front door of the school, I felt every eye within viewing distance staring at me. It is a small town, so if you're new everybody knows it. Of course, the chattering whispers began and I could hear it all. They thought they were quiet but with my hearing I could hear everything crystal clear.

"Holy shit, man. Look at that."

"New girl's hot."

"Who the hell is that?"

"Where did she come from?"

So on and so forth. I just smirked and kept walking. The control I had on my powers allowed me to reduce the range of my hearing, so I minimized my hearing. To avoid catching any more eyes with my own, I pulled out my phone and opened up my schedule and locker number, as if I hadn't already memorized them. I just hate that awkward look away thing, you know what I mean?

As I was closing my locker, I jumped at the sight of two people standing in front of me.

"Annie, right?" asked the boy.

"Yeah," I said, cautiously.

"Sorry if we scared you," he chuckled. "The people here are so friggin' antisocial. They will talk about you all day but not to your face. We figured we would break the ice once we heard you were starting. I'm Miguel and this is Emily."

"Hey. What's up? See you found your locker alright," said Emily, picking up where Miguel left off.

"Yeah, it wasn't too hard. Nice to meet you guys," I said, feeling nervous and unsure of where this conversation was going.

"So you're Nick's little sister right? Winters?" Emily asked.

Cousins, technically. "Yes, I am. You guys know him?" I asked, relieved.

"Of course!" she laughed. "He was pretty popular around here."

"I'm not surprised."

Nick is the kind of guy that most guys want to be: dirty blond hair, crystal blue eyes, tall, strong, and very handsome. Not to mention he was, and still is, a genuinely good guy. And he practically raised me. So you can imagine why he would be so popular in school.

Emily started walking and Miguel and I followed. "How come we haven't seen you around? Did you go somewhere else?"

"No, I uh … I was homeschooled." *Not a complete lie.*

"Oh, really? Hmm, cool." Miguel looked me over trying, and failing, to be discreet. "Where do you have class?" he asked as I caught his eyes, actually trying to make eye contact now.

"Umm," I pulled out my phone again, "Mrs. Farrell, room 109. So that way, I think," I said, pointing down the hall.

Emily jumped with excitement and smiled. "Yup! Same as me! Let's do this."

Let me tell you about these lovely people. Emily is a little shorter than myself (I am 5'3" if you're wondering). And she wore so many layers of clothes I wasn't sure if it would end. I mean, she looks like she jumped out of an art school made entirely of rainbows. She has dark red hair pushed up into a messy bun and seems to have a permanent smile plastered on her face. It was as if my arrival was the best news she had ever heard. I liked her almost immediately.

Miguel is your average joe. He has short, dark hair that spikes up in the front. His tan skin accents his beautiful brown eyes. That first day he wore a T-shirt, basketball shorts, and the oldest sneakers I had ever seen. He is kind and possesses this calming voice that could probably make anyone feel re-laxed.

The first half of the school day went smoothly. I made it to all my classes and was really starting to like Emily and Miguel. After lunch, we had some free time and wandered the hallway talking. I was so used to hearing chatter about me at that point of the day and my name floating around that I didn't hear him calling me until he said my birth name.

"Annie James," he whispered.

I stopped mid-sentence and turned around. There were only about six people who knew my real name. This particular person was David Hunter. He stood in the middle of the hall-way, everyone parting around him as if there was an invisible bubble surrounding him. For a fifteen-year-old boy, he was tall. Olive skin made his green eyes pop. Everyone stopped to watch. Apparently, even *they* knew something was going to go down.

He stood there with fists clenched, shoulders tensed, his buddies close behind him. Miguel lightly grabbed my arm.

"Annie, walk away," panic was clear in his tone. "He will..."

"I know him," I interrupted. I locked eyes with David and started to walk toward him. I heard Miguel and Emily's hearts racing. Everybody's actually. I minimized my hearing again. "David!" I blurted out nervously. "Long time no see. How've you been?" I smiled. There was no way I would let him see how scared I really was, which was a decent amount.

"I am doing fantastic now." His smile was purely diabolical, nothing fantastic about it. His eyes sparkled with excitement.

"Well I'm glad to hear I can still make your day," I said with as much sarcasm as I could.

"I've waited years to see you again. I have most definitely missed you."

"Funny. I didn't miss you at all." That was all it took. He charged up to me, grabbed me by my neck, and pinned me to the wall of lockers. I hit his arm out of the way and kicked him in the stomach throwing him back. I went to punch him but he grabbed my fist with his other hand, punched me in the stomach, then kicked my face. I fell to the ground, a piercing pain shooting through my head and down to my stomach. Back and forth.

He started kicking me repeatedly, my back to the wall. Finally, after many failed attempts to stop him, I caught his leg and pulled him down. As I pulled myself up and looked around I noticed people's mouths hanging wide open, and teachers were just watching. *Why aren't they stopping it?* I thought. The most effort I saw was Emily, Miguel, and maybe two teachers yelling.

"Dave, stop!"

"That's enough, David!"

"Hunter!" But no one physically tried to intervene. David pushed himself off the ground with a grunt, and was now even more pissed off than before. I managed to block a few more hits before he pinned me against the wall of lockers again, combination locks jabbing into my back.

"Stop fighting, Annie." He leaned in, putting his mouth to my ear. "No one will help you. Everyone knows who my father is. It's you and me. I've been waiting a long time for you."

"Go to hell, David." I spat in his face and he kneed me, hard, causing a coughing fit.

"You'll get what you deserve."

"I was ten, David! Ten! I had no control." I pushed against him and he pinned me down harder, his strength overwhelming.

He got even quieter and more serious than he had been moments before. "You have a clean slate right now. No one knows who you are. But I do; I know *what* you are, Annie. So if you continue to fight me, I will tell them. All of them."

"Please no," I begged. School was a chance to live a semi-normal life. I had a growing fear in the pit of my stomach and a river of tears waiting to flow.

"I can ruin you right here, right now. Is that what you want?" I looked at him with boiling hatred. "Hmm? Is it?" He pressed on my wrists. I looked down and shook my head. "No?" he asked.

"No," I said defeatedly.

"Well then, let's finish this." He backed up. "Okay guys," he said to his gang, who now walked over and dragged me outside. Stinging tears found their way out as I glared at David.

Then it began: a good, solid beating. Each moment longer than the last. I didn't fight and I didn't talk. At the end, as my body was pulsing with pain, the boys backed off and Dave leaned next to me, putting his hand behind my head, holding it up. I moved away but he just did it again with more force.

"Sh sh sh. Come on now. One simple sentence and the whole school will know," I sat still. "It was good to finally see you again," he said, laughing. "I can't wait to tell my dad that you are here."

As he stood up I began to gasp. "Wait. No, no, no!" I reached out as if I could stop him and he fed me a final blow. I felt the fear envelope me as I blacked out.

3
IT'S OKAY RIGHT?

I woke up in the nurse's office; I reached up to my lip, swollen. My eyebrow was cut open, but a strip held it together. I was about to leave when the nurse came back in. "Miss Winters." I nodded slowly; I was in a daze, still thinking about what had just happened, but I began to heave myself off the bed. "Annie, where are you going?" I stared at her. "You do realize you were just severely beaten right?"

"Yeah... yeah I remember that." *Does she think I'm stupid?* "I'm fine though. Honestly, don't worry. Thank you for taking care of me but I have to go."

"Woah there!" She chuckled kindly. "Listen, it's my job to keep you here until a parent or guardian comes to get you. I called your house and someone is coming."

I smiled at her but answered with doubt. "Who answered?" I looked at her. "My father? He isn't coming, ma'am. Thank you though. I really have to get home."

"Annie, I can't let you leave. What if something happens?"

All I could think was that something had already happened and no one stopped it.

Miguel interrupted poking his head through the door, "Mrs. P, we'll take her home. We're heading that way anyway. It's no problem."

"I'm not suppos..." I looked straight at her, the look on my face saying I was going to leave anyway. "Alright, feel better, Miss Winters, but this won't happen again," she said with a stern face. *Don't hold your breath.* "Miguel, tell your father I say hello."

"Will do, Mrs. P."

"Thank you, guys. I would have never been able to leave," I told Emily and Miguel as we quickly walked away from the office.

"It was no problem," Emily said. "Also, Miguel's father owns an emergency health clinic and the supply company that supplies the school, so she loves Miguel."

"That is incredibly helpful," I stated.

"Anyway, how are you feeling?" Miguel said, changing the subject back to me.

"I'm alright. In quite a bit of pain but dealing. Does David do that to every new student?"

"Most of them, if he sees fit. Although he never beats on anyone the way he did to you. Emily and I are surprised you can walk!"

"Yeah he and I had a kind of a, um, *falling out* in the past."

"I had a feeling you two knew each other," Miguel said. "Seriously though, I've never seen him beat on anyone so hard. Especially having super strength! Woah!"

"Wait. You guys know he is a Power?" I was utterly shocked. Powers aren't allowed to be in school. Hence me not putting that on my already forged entry papers.

"Of course! Don't you know who his father is?" *Oh I know him.* "Joshua Hunter basically owns this county. He has essentially had the U.S. government in his pocket since he stopped the Triad. David can do whatever he wants without getting in trouble. The authorities are practically controlled by his father." Anger seeped into me. Reminding me that my parents' killer was looked at as a national hero.

"That's why there are never any Powers here," Emily explained. "As soon as they arrive and are found out, Josh Hunter gets them. It's actually really messed up. It's not like they aren't people too."

I looked at them, feeling a little more comfortable. *Maybe I could tell them. They might be cool with it, but I can't. They could get hurt.* "So you two have nothing against Powers?"

"Nope." "Not at all," they said simultaneously, grinning at each other.

"Interesting," I said, but really what I meant was HELL YEAH!! Considering how friendly they were from the get-go, I guess it wasn't surprising that they'd be accepting. "Most people in this town are haters. I mean I know my father is and he talks about it constantly. How are the students about it?"

"Honestly there are a few who don't care either way, but most of them are Joshua Hunter supporters. So, you know what *that* means," Emily said with disgust.

"It's terrible." When we arrived at my house, we all stood there for a second. "Well anyways guys, thank you so much for bringing me home and breaking the ice today."

"It was no problem at all, sweetie. I'm sorry David was so extra horrible," Emily said.

"Well, it's certainly not your fault. So, I'll see you tomorrow?" I asked hopefully.

"Absolutamente!" Miguel assured.

"Feel better, Annie." They walked away and I sighed while looking at my front door knowing that my awful uncle was waiting inside.

I took a deep breath. "Here we go." I walked in and closed the door as quietly as I could.

"Annie!" *Crap, he heard me.*

"Brett." Even though he wasn't anything like my father, he insisted I call him Dad around company. He didn't want anyone asking questions if people came over. God forbid they find out my real parents were Powers. I refused to call him Dad otherwise.

See, my uncle was raised in a household with two loving parents. However, they favored my mother. Not purposefully excluding him but planting a seed of envy and hate for Powers. Once Brett got married at age 22 to a woman named Heather, he cut off contact with my mom. Until me. Heather and my uncle had four kids, including Nick. Once I came to live with them, Brett quickly became abusive toward me, especially once I got my powers, and Heather couldn't watch it anymore. She divorced him and in turn he resented me even more. Brett refused to let me be around his other children. Heather fought him, but I told her I wanted to be with Nick anyway, so I stayed.

Not my smartest decision.

"What the hell is wrong with you? It's your first day and already I got a phone call. Why do you think I never allowed this?"

"I'm sorry."

"What were you thinking?" he yelled, his face red.

"It wasn't my fault. David goes to school there and he..."

"I don't care what David does! He knows about you and that's dangerous enough. Does anyone else?" he screamed, towering over me.

I looked down, rolling my eyes. "No, I let him beat me."

"Good. Keep it that way."

"But he shouldn't be allowed t..." He slapped me, my already bruised face aching.

A moment of silence.

"Keep it that way, Annie." He said my name as if it were a disease.

I held my hand to my cheek. "Okay." I walked up to my room and closed the door lightly. I didn't want to give him another reason to yell.

"Fuck." I sat on my bed and pulled my legs to my chest. "Why me?" Then I heard an argument from downstairs. Nick had come home, and I could hear the muffled yelling between him and my uncle.

"Your sister already messed up. The little shit got in a fight today."

"Wait, Annie? What happened?" asked Nick concernedly.

"The Hunter kid found her; honestly, she needs some good beatings."

Nick started coming upstairs, calling back calmly but firmly, "She did nothing to you, Dad. Seriously, you need to lay off." He lightly knocked on my door. "Ann, it's me."

22

"Come in," I said softly. He walked in. All six feet of him. His dirty blond hair a tidy mess, his strong arms showing remnants of working in his auto shop all day. There were a few days' worth of scruff on his face, which of course only made him look better. Finally, his crystal blue eyes landed on me. "Hey. Holy shit." I hadn't changed yet, so he saw my blood-covered clothes.

"It's nothing," I said as I grabbed new clothes, "really."

"Look at me." I turned around. "I'm sorry I couldn't help." He pulled me into his arms and held me. "Are you okay?" I nodded. "I mean are you *okay*?"

"I don't know what I expected. Really I don't."

"Did anything good happen?"

"Yeah I made two friends actually. They seem like the only decent people at that whole school."

"See! And they picked the best person to recruit them!"

"Ha ha, very funny. How was your day?"

"Oh the power to my apartment went out. I need a new generator. That's why I'm here. I'm dirty as hell and I can't shower in the dark. So, I will be home for a little bit if you need me. Okay?"

"Yeah. I love you, Nick."

"You better!" He smiled, leaving the room.

"Wait!" I racing toward him to get to the shower before he could. After showering, I climbed into bed, covering myself with the sheets as if they could make the world disappear. The bullshit of today was over. Thank God.

4
MIRROR OF MY PAST

Standing in front of the mirror, I recreated the bruises and scratches. Overnight they had healed completely but I could not go into school without any bruises. After that kind of beating, having no marks at all would give me away immediately. The most basic ability a Power has is rapid healing. Luckily, I had enough control over my body that I could do the reverse as well. *This is gonna be a long day, I can feel it. A long week, actually,* I thought.

David continued bullying me for the rest of the week. Every. Single. Day. In the bathroom, the parking lot, the hallway. Guess what I did? Nothing. It was infuriating. That's how my week went. Fan-friggin'-tastic and it only got better.

After school Friday, once I finished saying goodbye to Miguel and Emily, I walked home and all was quiet, which was weird, with it being Friday and all. Out of nowhere a black SUV pulled up next to me. It looked like it should have been carrying the president, but instead of the president, two men jumped out and grabbed me while a third injected me with a needle full of some sort of clear liquid; I was going numb and starting to black out. I would have fought back, but this all happened in a matter of four seconds so, you know, I didn't really have a huge window.

❋ ❋ ❋

I woke up strapped to a table in a room full of computers and glass chambers with industrial-sized cables leading to each one. Everything shone with cleanliness, organized with impeccable scrutiny. *What the heck kind of lab is this?* The chambers looked like they could comfortably fit maybe five people in each of them. They were a little too big for lab rats—at least of the rodent variety. *So what is going on here?* Unless … "Oh no," I said under my breath. Then I saw him. I had only seen him two other times and neither were great memories. Now he stood right in front of me. In the flesh. I could feel the anger building inside of me. Heat flared as blood flushed my face.

He was smiling. "Hello, Miss James."

"Josh," I said through clenched teeth.

Joshua Hunter was a tall, and well featured man. It seemed he had fair skin, yet it was somehow perfectly tanned. His dark hair was combed neatly back with slight stubble around his mouth and chin, flawlessly manicured. Not a scar or blemish in sight. He had this noble arrogance about him. Although, if you knew him at all, you could see the ugly evil shine right through his immaculately white smile. You felt as though his blue-hazel eyes could see right through you. Ugh, it gives me chills just thinking about it. Not the good kind of chills either. That day he was wearing black pants with a deep red button up topped with a black tie. Everything flawlessly

25

tailored to his fit condition. Yeah, he even dressed the part of the evil douchebag.

"It has been far too long has it not?" he said.

"Not long enough," I said, seething with anger. He chuckled, clearly pushing aggravation aside. I was already getting under his skin — good. He cleared his throat.

"Well, you are here now. Conveniently enough your P.T. is the same as your mother's. Less work for me."

Ah, P.T., my power tranquilizer. It is used to knock out my abilities, temporarily. Some P.T.'s are Power specific, but not all. I rolled my eyes. "Yeah, lucky for you," I dead panned.

His face changed and he looked me dead in the eyes. He was so close I could see the patterns in the color of his eyes. "This insolence is going to have to stop if you expect to be released. However, if it continues, I would be more than happy to teach you the proper way to behave. What is your decision, Miss James?"

Pulling my face out of his grip, I looked away and didn't say a word. "Good girl." He approached the computer, to which the table I was tied to was connected. "Now my work can begin." He typed something into the touch screen and the table tilted back horizontally, so now I was parallel to the floor.

"Wait, what are you doing?"

"My job," he said with a cavernous grin. It was like a game to him.

"Just let me go, Josh. I'm older now and stronger. I could take you out!"

"*Take me out?* Very funny! Yet so incredibly naïve."

I struggled against the restraints. "You have no idea what I am capable of."

"Oh? Well then let us see, shall we?" He waved his

hand and the restraints released me. "If you can get past me, you will be free to go." He stood like a gentleman with one arm behind his back. *Who is he trying to fool?*

I got off the table and lifted my hand, but as soon as I started charging up, he shot my hand with his powers, making me lose my concentration. I screamed in frustration, and slight pain. Being hit with someone's powers was like an electric shock. Depending on the strength of the power, it could be much worse.

"If you expect to leave you are going to have to be much quicker than that."

I immediately started shooting back at him. One shot after the other, but he blocked every attempt and then shot me in the stomach. I flew against the wall. The shots, which looked like strands of light, flew from our fingertips.

Strands of blue light, like lightning, that hurt like hell.

"Strong enough, Annie?" He shot again. "What? Can you not fight back?" I raised my hand but he pushed it back again with powers of his own. I could hardly breathe with the effort. "Come now, I thought you were stronger!"

I watched as his palms lit up and his fingers started to glow. Such extreme power. The light flew toward me and I hit the wall once again, but this time he didn't stop. It ran through me like electricity. His face changed to a type of determination. And hope?

"Please.... Josh.... Sto..."

"Stop!" She came out of nowhere. Like, literally I think she just appeared. At least that's what it felt like. And let me tell you, Josh stopped right away and I sunk quickly to the floor.

"Ursula, my love! I was not anticipating that your arrival would be so soon." I had read of her cruelty, while I researched, but never her beauty. Stories of her were like ghosts in the background. Long, curled, dark brown hair that draped across her shoulders. Eyes the color of emeralds and eyebrows perfectly manicured to a curve. The curves of her face so symmetrical she had reached perfection. She walked with a sort of elegance. If in a room of crowded people, she would be the person to make everyone go silent with just her presence. I mean, even Josh shut up for her.

"I couldn't possibly miss this reunion," she said gazing at me as she walked to Josh. "Hello, darling," she cooed, wrapping her arms around his neck, kissing him deeply. The kiss of evil I tell you.

"My goodness!" She walked toward me, on the floor and holding my stomach, crying in pain. "You are more beautiful than I imagined." I pushed myself closer to the wall. "Oh please child, I just want to get to know you. I've waited so long." She reached her hand out to touch my face and I pushed it away, cowering against the wall. After what Josh had just done, I didn't want anyone touching me. That's not how she saw it. Her power was palpable, the air rippled around her as she appeared right in front of me. She grabbed my face and whispered in my ear, her long-polished nails digging into my skin. "There is no need to be rude, Annie. Respect is incredibly important and honestly I expected more from you." I nodded quickly. She was so strong, I thought my jaw was going to shatter from her touch alone. "Good, my child, very good. You'll learn your manners here, right my darling?"

"Yes, she will." Josh assured. They shared another kiss.

"However, maybe you will join us. You are our little orphan Annie after all," she chuckled, her green eyes beaming with excitement.

"Fuck you." I knew that had been a mistake right away.

Her head turned toward me and, as her dark hair settled on her shoulders, I watched her eyes turn a dark yellow. I fell to the floor. I couldn't move. The pain was immobilizing. It felt like my bones and veins were on fire. I tried to scream but my lungs wouldn't allow it.

"I don't think you are understanding. You see, Annie, there are rules. I am your superior, therefore you will respect me." She leaned over me. "Do you hear me?"

"Yes!" I forced out. Her mental grip loosening just enough to allow me to speak. "Please. Stop! I'm sorry. I am so sorry!" She released me and I rolled onto my side. I tasted blood. *What was that?*

"As long as that is clear, you have nothing to fear from me." She smiled as if the past minute had never happened. *Crazy bitch*, I thought. But I had learned my lesson and did not say it out loud.

She hadn't lifted a finger. Her eyes held all the power. Since a Power's powers increase with age, I had to assume that, with that much power, she must be old as hell. Or from hell. One or the other.

"I've always wanted a daughter of my own." She looked at me admiringly. *Hell no!* I thought. *I will die before I'm associated with you*, but instead I held back tears. I was shaking as she ran her finger down my cheek. I didn't dare move. "How would you feel about making this your home? Hmm?" I didn't answer. "Oh, come now, Annie. Don't be scared to answer. I won't bite." *Oh no of course not, but you'll light my insides on fire.* I looked at her. *What will she do if she doesn't like my response?*

"Well? Would you like it?"

29

"No. I wouldn't." I saw anger flash ever so briefly in her eyes.

"Very well. Honesty is the best policy. And quite frankly, I have a friend that may be able to persuade you. Joshua, darling, contact our Mind Bender. You'll get used to it here, Annie. However, it will have to be without me, I have some business to attend to. Au revoir!" She and Josh said their goodbye, with another kiss, then, with a huge gust of wind, she was gone and I was left with *him*.

"Okay, Miss James, back to work."

5
ELECTRICITY

Of course after that it got no better. I struggled as he dragged me to another table, different than the first. This one was attached to one of the chambers, so that the table could slide right into it.

"Let me go, Josh! Just let me friggin' go!" I didn't want any more of this bullshit torture or whatever it was. However, Josh was having none of *my* bullshit. He grabbed my neck hard, picking me up and slamming me into the table. His eyes were filled with frustration and anger. What a temper.

"You only have about this much of my patience left, Annie," he said, his fingers an inch apart, "and then you are no longer going to receive any leniency from me. If you expect to leave here before the weekend ends, then you had better behave."

"By the end of the *weekend*," I said horrified. *A whole weekend of this?!*

The restraints strapped themselves around me as he slammed his hands onto the table angrily. "This can either be extremely or mildly painful; the decision is yours. But I will not tolerate your impertinence and disobedience. Do you understand?"

What could he possibly need from me for an entire weekend? What would he do?

"Miss James?!" His voice seemed to echo through my head.

"Okay. Okay," I huffed. The table lifted and slid into the glass chamber.

"Good girl." Wires came out from the table and Josh walked in and started attaching them to my skin. "Now you be still, or this will hurt more than it needs to, my dear." He smiled, clearly hoping that I *would* move, and walked back to the computer screen. The chamber closed as he tapped something into the screen and then I felt it—needles coming out from the table and jabbing into my arms, from the center of my hands to my shoulders.

I screamed as I had never screamed before. I had thought being beaten by David had hurt, but this was so much worse. The needles were positioned less than an inch apart and there must have been at least thirty in each arm. You know what Josh did? He stood there smiling like he was watching his favorite movie. A man like that belongs in an asylum. I mean, honestly, what brings someone to this point of crazy?

"What the hell are these for? Oh my God!"

"You will grow accustomed to it. I'm referring to the pain, of course. This particular test is not going to be repeated."

"This is a test?" I asked through utter shock.

"I have to find your pressure points." I leaned my head

32

back, closed my eyes and tensed up. "Slowly but surely you are learning. It is not too difficult, is it?"

Yeah, if you're terrified. I quickly nodded instead.

"Now let us begin."

I had read about pressure points. They were used by Hunters to temporarily neutralize a Power's powers. So I don't know why I didn't expect it, but as he said that, electricity ran through me. I felt it push though my body from each of the needles. He watched in joy as I screamed. *Bastard.* It continued pulsing at my wrists for a while, finding where in my body my powers originated. I couldn't think or see straight. I thought it couldn't get any worse but of course I had thought too soon. At the spot on each wrist where the electricity had centralized, a thick piece of metal with a few blinking lights wrapped around, like a bracelet. Once it locked in place a laser-type light pierced through my skin and remained there.

I would have screamed, if not for the rush of nausea quickly taking over. It hurt more than you can imagine, but that wasn't all. My powers drained; I felt them go. *Holy freaking crap, was this how the weekend would continue?*

6
LET ME OUTTA HERE

It had been two days and nothing had improved. It was continuous experimentation all weekend, injections of all different combinations. Painful combinations. I was exhausted to say the least and now this?

"Sir, someone is at the front door. I think it's her brother."

"Nick?! No, Josh. No, please." I could deal with this torture but Nick wouldn't live through it. No mortal human could endure this kind of pain.

"Ah, Nick Winters here to join the party? Excellent!" He started walking out, his face bright with devilish excitement.

"Josh!" I screamed at him. "Please, you can do anything to me. Josh, please!" I was desperate, but he just smiled and walked out.

"Damn it." At this point I was off the table but still in the chamber, like a friggin' cage. I still had the container brace-

lets in, and let me tell you something about them: ow, okay?
Just ow.

7

NICK

I was pacing back and forth at the front door to Josh's building. "Josh, you son of a bitch! Come on." The door opened; he seemed unreal in his tailored suit. His longish hair perfectly combed back.

"Mr. Winters, how nice of you to visit. How can I help you?" With a condescending smile he looked me over.

"Cut the shit, Josh. I know she's in there."

"Who?" Clearly he just wanted to piss me off and unfortunately I couldn't help but fall into it.

"She's sixteen, Josh. Sixteen! She doesn't deserve this. Give her to me." I was so tense. I was two seconds away from punching him in the Goddamn face. He was still smiling. "My sister, Josh! Annie! Where the hell is she?! Let me see her."

He finished laughing at me and turned around, "Well why did you not simply say so in the first place? Come. Join me." I shot him a look that I wish could kill.

We walked down a few hallways and then downstairs where we entered a massive room with testing chambers and blinking lights and screens.

"Annie!" *Oh thank God, but how can I get her out?* Then two guys came up to me and knocked me down with a well-placed punch to the stomach. They trained their weapons on me, guns aimed at my head.

8

UNBEARABLE

"Nick! No. No!" *He's not a Power. It's illegal to do this.*
"Josh, I'll do anything. Please."

"Miss James, must I remind you of your place here?"

"No. No you don't," I said, willing to say anything to
protect Nick. Even if that meant somehow keeping my mouth
shut.

"Josh, listen, she's too young. Please let me bring her
home," Nick said as two guns were brought closer to his head,
giving me a minor heart attack.

"It has been a while, Nicholas. Now you think I am just
going to allow you to leave? So soon?"

"Fuck you, Hunter." One of the goons hit Nick with
the butt of his gun.

"Stop! Just stop it!" I screamed.

"What did I tell you, Annie?" Josh said unfeelingly.

"I don't give a shit what you say. Keep your disgusting

hands off of him."

"Very well then," he said, returning to the computer. "We will start with 75 milliamps. Yes?"

"Now hold up ... AHHHH!" I fell to the floor of the chamber, trying to scream. *Come on, Annie,* I thought, *Nick is watching.* However, I couldn't move or speak. I couldn't breathe! My body began twitching on its own and a terrible burning feeling flew through me.

"Fuck! Stop it!" Nick yelled, desperation in his eyes.

The shock stopped. Breathing heavily, I pushed myself to my knees the best I could, but my movements were strained and painful. I knew it was hurting Nick to see this. But Josh wasn't satisfied.

"What else do you need her for? Huh?" asked Nick. "What other tests could you possibly have?"

"Actually we are more or less done for now." Josh said with a smirk. *He is just playing games.*

"Okay, then let her go," Nick said hopefully. "Let her come with me."

Josh opened the chamber and I cautiously stepped out. When he released the bracelets, I screamed and fell to my knees, holding my wrists; blood flowed down my hands from the holes the lasers had made.

"You want her, Nicholas. Here she is. Oh! One more thing." He turned around with a gun and shot me in the chest. I was out like a light yet again.

9
TRUTH?

I woke up in my bed at home. Nick must have carried me there. I couldn't believe Josh had let me go and I couldn't help but wonder what the hell he had shot me with. I got off the bed and held my head in my hands. Everything was healed, so at least I wasn't in pain. However, a sort of dread still lurked in my mind and an anxiety still pressed on my chest.

"Oh my God." Nick hugged me with all his strength.

"Hey, Nick," I said through the pressure. It was good to be in his arms. I closed my eyes and held him close.

"I'm so sorry. I didn't know where you were."

"How could you? Are you okay?" I put my hand on his face where he now had a nice bruise.

"Of course I am." He smiled.

"I'm sorry I can't heal you."

"I'm fine, Ann. Really. I've had worse bruises from work."

"It's Monday isn't it?" I asked.

"Yeah."

"Well I need to be in school then," I grabbed some clothes.

"Come on, Annie. I think you can miss one day. I mean really."

"Nick, if I miss a day, they win. I won't let them control my life."

He looked at me with his piercing blue eyes and said, "Okay, sis. Alright. There is no chance you'll change your mind, is there?"

"No," I said smiling. "There isn't."

"Okay. I will drive you."

"I can walk. You need rest."

"I am going to take you." I rolled my eyes jokingly but nodded. "Come here, kid," he said, pulling me in and hugging me again. "I love you. Don't ever forget that." I loved him too. "Let's go," he said, pulling me back from the hug.

❖ ❖ ❖

I sighed as we arrived at school and then kissed Nick on the cheek. "How would I do this without you?"

He smiled, "You don't need me. Now go on. Get."

I walked up to the door and steeled myself. *Here we go.*

I checked in at the front desk and went to class. Of course I received huge hugs from my two new friends. We had a whisper conversation just to catch up. Of course I did not inform them of the type of weekend I truly had. I'm just glad Josh hadn't involved them.

When the bell rang to end the day, the hallway turned into a war zone, with the pushing, shoving and screaming—you know how it is. High school. Then I saw him, the spawn of

Satan. He was beating on someone else today. I guess he had had a boring weekend. But beating on a normal human? *That just won't do.*

"Hey! Dave!" I yelled in my moment of bravery.

He looked up, still holding onto the kid with his hand. "Oh! Annie! I thought you weren't here today. I'm happy you are though." He dropped the kid like a brick and waved a hand to his boys. They came toward me and this, my friends, is when I realized I kinda really fucked up. *At least the other kid will be okay*, I thought.

"Well I'm here. Do you seriously have nothing better to do?"

He laughed. "There *is* nothing better," he said cracking his knuckles. "It releases bad energy." He went to punch me, I grabbed his arm and punched his stomach. Then I blocked the two guys coming toward me with my arms and tripped one to the ground with my leg. Dave went for another punch but this time he got me right in the face and the other two charged at me as I recovered, pinning me to the wall. Dave delivered blows to my stomach one after another but the one to my face dropped me. I watched blood hit the ground and then heard someone walk toward us.

"Cut it out!" It was Miguel.

"Please, Miguel, no." I said as loudly as I could … so not loudly at all, considering I hadn't caught my breath yet. David laughed and ignored him.

"Hey, pendejo," Miguel continued, "leave her alone, you did enough last week."

David sighed as if a gnat had been flying around him. "Shaun, hold her," he said to one of his guys before leaving me and walking over to Miguel. "Listen here, *amigo*, I don't want to hurt you, so how about you shut the hell up and walk away."

"What did she do to you? Seriously, man. She had her initiation, so let her be." Miguel was standing his ground. Impressively brave, but he really should have stopped. Dave kneed him in the stomach.

"You're intimidated by him? What a joke!" I called.

He turned around, pissed that I had interrupted. After that, a few people yelled at him to stop kicking me but of course he didn't listen to them. Someone up there must have loved me though, because he did stop. He fell back holding his hands to his head.

"No. Damn it! Come on!" he yelled, punching a locker. It was as if someone had told him to stop. He looked at me like it was my fault and stormed off with his little posse following him. Then it happened to me.

It felt like someone had split my skull open and crawled into my head. "You are welcome, Miss James. See you soon." *He's in my head now?! Wonderful.*

Emily and Miguel ran over to me to help me up. I needed to talk to them. They lifted me up and as we walked I started to feel better, my body already beginning the healing process. "I need to tell you guys something, okay? Can we find a quiet place?"

"Yeah. Sure," Miguel said, glancing at Emily.

We found an empty room and I closed the door. "What I'm going to tell you can't leave this room, okay?"

"Okay. Are you alright?" Emily asked.

"Yeah, I'm fine. Well, depending on your definition of fine. So you guys know what Powers are? Well obviously. I mean duh." *Okay, take a breath, Ann. They aren't the ones to be worried about.* I was so nervous; my heart was in my throat. "I know you guys are worried about me getting beat up constantly but you don't have to be. Because I am a Power."

Miguel threw his hands up, walking in a victorious circle. "I knew it! I knew you were too hot to be a plain old human. Woohoo! Hell yeah!" Emily and I stood there smiling, staring at him. "I mean uh, really? How's that working out for you?" he backtracked, his face blushing, muttering something under his breath in Spanish.

I chuckled lovingly. "Um, actually not too great. You see I have these two fantastic friends starting to stand up for me and I'm concerned."

"Wait. Why? Just because you're a Power doesn't mean you deserve that shit," Emily argued.

"I know, Em, and let me tell you, I appreciate that more than you can imagine. But if you guys were to get hurt because of me, I could never forgive myself."

"Aww, Ann, he won't kill us or anything. We're all good," Miguel said matter of factly.

"Yeah, seriously. There is a line," Emily agreed.

I looked down, playing with my thumbs. "I know he won't *kill* you, but that's not the point. I don't want him laying a *finger* on you. This will be the only other favor I ask of you other than to keep this under wraps. The school thinks I'm human; if they find out, I might not be able to come back. If I let David beat me up, he isn't beating on someone else."

"You can't be serious. You would take that every day?" Miguel exclaimed.

"Of course I would. How can I let him do that to others, when the next day I will be healed?"

"Wow. You just keep getting hotter," Miguel said, causing Emily to hit him.

"Oh shut up," she said to Miguel. "Annie, if that's what you need, I think we can do that. Right Mig?"

"Okay fine," he said. "But if he says anything to me I'm punching him en los cojones, then running."

I smiled and shook my head. "If that's the best I can get from you I'll take it." I was so happy they would be safe now. Well, safer. That day ended with a nice hug. Better than a blackout right?

10
WELCOME HOME

"Ow, ow, ow," I said as Miguel and Emily helped lift me up after a particularly bad beating. *Is that my bone?* I thought, as I brought my arm into view. My eyes widened.

"It's okay, Ann," Miguel consoled. "I know what to do."

"No hospitals," I reminded. "I don't need anything. It will heal soon."

"No hospital," he confirmed. "And will you just let us help!"

We all walked to Miguel's house, a five-minute walk from school. Ten today because I could barely walk, now realizing that along with my fractured wrist, my leg was probably broken.

"You sure about this?" I asked, my anxiety telling me to run and hide.

"I am sure," Mig answered.

"Sweetie, Mig's dad is the nicest person you will ever

meet. It's gonna be alright," Emily pitched in. "I promise."

We turned a corner and walked up to an absolutely beautiful home. The grass was greener than any I'd ever seen. The flowers were placed in perfect succession. The house itself was two levels and built utilizing different kinds of stone.

"My mom is very specific about how the lawn looks," Miguel commented on seeing me eyeing the yard.

"It's wonderful," I responded.

"Until you step on the grass," he chuckled.

The smell of cooking food flooded us as we walked through the front door.

"Hello!" Miguel announced. A few short responses from other rooms greeted him. "Papi?"

"I'm in my office," a man's voice, with a slight hint of an accent, responded.

"Be right back," Miguel told us.

Emily and I looked at each other. She just mouthed "it's okay" to me. Rationally I knew if Miguel was as accepting as he seemed, his family had to be somewhat like him. But as a Power who had been locked in her room for half her life, and in a world where we are killed for sport, I was panicking.

Miguel and his father came walking to us a few minutes later.

"Emily! Welcome home, muñeca," he hugged her. "And this must be Annie. It is nice to meet you."

"It's my pleasure, Mr. Alvarez."

"Oh none of that! It's Enrique," he said, shaking my good hand.

"Alright you two," he said to Mig and Em, "you go ahead and wait in the family room, alright?" They both nodded, reassuringly. "You can come on over here with me, Annie." I could see where Miguel got his calm disposition. His dad had the same welcoming and calming voice.

"Listen, Dr. Alvarez… "

"Por favor, Annie, you can absolutely call me Enrique. And before you go on, let me just say, you are completely safe in this house. Miguel told me what you are dealing with," he paused. "Now as far as this is concerned," gesturing toward my wrist, "you know this is a compound fracture. Don't you?"

"Yeah. The bone kind of gave that one away."

He chuckled. "Tell me, how does the healing process work for you? Normally, I would be sending you into surgery for this. I am sure it comes as a shock, but I don't get any Powers at the clinic."

"I can't imagine you would," I returned with a chuckle of my own. "Honestly, it will be healed in a few hours and I'll hardly feel it healing at all. Allegedly our bodies numb the surrounding nerves so no pain can be felt during the healing process. I mean, all I feel now is a deep ache. But not really intense pain."

"Incredible."

"Yeah… " I said, looking down at my hands. Really incredible. It doesn't mean it isn't excruciating while it happens. *If I weren't a Power, I wouldn't even have to be healing from anything right now.*

"Is there anything at all I can do to speed up the process?"

"Nothing, sir." He gave me a "you know you don't have to call me that" look.

"I know Miguel just wants to help, always incredibly insistent that boy. But since there is really nothing I can do for you, I am sure you want to clean up at least."

"That would be wonderful."

"Escucha, I would like you to stay for dinner. I have left some towels in the bathroom. They will be thrown away once you're done so don't worry about the blood. You can clean up and come to the dining room and relax. Once dinner is over, and your wrist is healed, I will wrap it up and no one at school will know that it's healed. Sound fair?"

"Oh you really don't have to do that. I will just clean up and head home."

"I insist! We believe the more the merrier at dinner time. Vamonos." We started walking out of his office and toward the bathroom. He guided me over and opened the door. "Towels over here, and once you're done just throw them in the second garbage there. Bueno?"

"Si, gracias."

"Ah! Muy bien! Y Annie?"

"Yes?"

"I hope I am not overstepping. But this town ... there are some terrible people in this town. And I see," he looked me over sympathetically, "that you have met some of these people. I want to assure you that I am not one of them. Whenever you need anything, my family will help you in whatever way we can."

I almost couldn't form words. His kindness toward me, for someone he had just met, was something I was definitely not accustomed to. "I appreciate your kindness. Thank you so much." *Don't cry, don't cry.*

I looked in the mirror to see something quite horrifying. "Oh dear heaven, Annie," I commented at myself, shaking my head. Wonderful first impression. Blood was dried on my face, having dripped from my broken nose and a cut on my forehead. I began washing it all off. The towels quickly becoming completely red. "Sorry," I mumbled out loud.

Once I was satisfied with my now only half haggard appearance, I walked toward the dining room. The walls of the hallway were lined with family photos, displaying the happy, normal moments a family should have. It made me happy to know that even in our crazy town, a bit of joy could still exist.

"Hey! You're gonna make me drop it!" I heard Miguel yell. Yet there was a hint of playfulness in his voice. Diego, Miguel's little brother, ran by. Meanwhile, Miguel held a huge bowl of paella.

Emily was already sitting at the table. She looked at me and patted the chair next to her. I gladly plopped down, finally off of my feet.

"Feel any better?" she asked.

"Do I look any better?" I laughed. "I'll be healed soon. All good." Then someone bumped into me on my other side.

"Gabriella! Manners, mija," Miguel's mom scolded, with more than just a trace of an accent in her voice.

"Sorry..." she said to me.

"It's quite alr..."

"Can you use your powers?" Gabriella blurted out.

"Gabby, stop it," Miguel said, annoyed, trying to bring the food over.

"Can you use them whenever you want?" Gabriella continued, clearly ignoring Mig.

"Actually, yeah. I can," I whispered.

"Can I see?"

"Only if you keep it between you and me."

"I swear!"

"You triple promise?"

"Yes, yes!"

"Alright." I kept my hand on my lap but let strands of light jump between my fingers.

"Woooooah."

I looked at her, putting my finger up to my lips. "Shh." She gestured zipping her lips and throwing away the key. Then she flew off the chair—no doubt to tell everyone what I'd shown her. I just smiled.

"Isn't she just adorable?" Emily commented.

"Unbearably."

I took it all in. The commotion of plates hitting the table, the smell of each dish. I was about to ask if I could help, but...

"Don't even bother. They won't let you lift a finger," Emily informed. I closed my mouth. "It's just what they are like." She and Mig had been friends since kindergarden. Emily's father had been abusive toward her mother and then abandoned them both. Her mother, a raging alcoholic, often left Emily to fend for herself. She spent most of her time at Mig's house; it was like her second home.

"I am Miguel's mamá," she came around the table and pulled me in, giving me the most affectionate hug. "Sofía." I'm telling you, this family is just a big love fest.

At last, they sat down for dinner. As soon as we finished praying, chaos continued. Everybody passing bowls around. Bumping into each other. But I found myself looking on in admiration. I had never had this. Not even the craziness of a simple family dinner. The aggravated comments as food spilled over plates. The sibling rivalry of who could eat more. It was beautifully crazy. I loved every moment.

✿ ✿ ✿

I sat back in my chair as full as I had ever been in my life. If they had asked me to have one more bite, I may have exploded.

"You three crazy kids, go hang out. The rest of us will clean up. Do you hear me, Gabby? That includes you," Mig's mom said.

"Mrs. Alvarez, please let me help," I insisted.

"Cariña, go relax," she insisted more forcefully.

"Come on, Ann," Miguel said.

I raised an eyebrow. "Alright."

My wrist only needed about an hour more to heal. So we all went to the basement and watched a movie. Nick had texted me while we were at dinner, so I let him know I was okay. Of course, not a peep from Brett. A small gift.

I mean, despite the clothes with droplets of blood on them, I felt like a normal teenage girl. I had friends. Real friends.

11

LEAP YEAR

And life went on in much the same vein. The whole first year followed this pattern. Many weekends Josh experimented on me and during the week I went to school, hung out with my friends, and was abused by David, really making me doubt my decision to even leave the house. Don't get me wrong. I didn't just take this abuse. I tried going to the cops. They blew me off. Saying that there was nothing they could do. Josh's influence had no end. Even though, as far as anyone in town knew, I wasn't a Power.

Some life I had. Right?

I spent the summer at home deep in the forests behind my house. I used the trees as targets for different kinds of powers. I enhanced my abilities nicely, despite the stationary targets. I made sure to sneak out when nobody was around. Josh only got me once the whole summer, but he kept me for two weeks. That, my friends, was horrible. He must have tried about twenty concoctions on me. But despite a little discomfort, none of them ended up being my Formula. Of course, because he was getting frustrated, he just electrocuted me here and there. My pain tolerance definitely grew during those two weeks.

The only reason I even got out was because on that given day my container bracelets shorted out when I was given shower time. It is safe to say I was escaping given that opportunity. But what I learned from Josh during that particular stay, was almost priceless....

It was spurred by a "What the hell is wrong with you?" question from yours truly.

"I was born a superlatively healthy, normal child. As all Powers are. The only exception, naturally, being an accelerated intelligence. By four years old I was beginning to read. So by the time I was six, my father was educating me about Powers. Books he and my grandfather had authored themselves. He would speak nearly every day of the abominations Powers were. How they took advantage of the world around them and created a danger in themselves. It was our family's job to eliminate them. Though the rest of the world remained largely unaware of Powers, my family had been killing them for centuries. It was our mission in life. So much so, my great grandfather changed our last name to Hunter."

My eyes remained locked on him, as he paced in front of my chamber.

"My father thought my intelligence was his doing. That I was a prodigy brought forth to 'Forward the Mission!' I hung on every word. At the age of nine I was learning to create Formulas. A hatred for Powers had grown within me so strongly that I longed for my first kill. I spent months learning the intri-

cacies of DNA. Learning how to strip away the extra base pair
a Power's DNA contains. A few days after my twelfth birthday I was working on my first Formula alone. Suddenly it felt
like my hands were on fire. I thought perhaps I had spilled a
chemical or something. Then my hands began to glow. I began
screaming and my father came running into the room. His face
turned from concern to lividity. I knew what this meant. I had
read about it a dozen times. I was getting powers. In front of
me was my father, a Power Hunter. I pleaded, but he grabbed
me and dragged me to a chamber and threw me inside. He left
me there for what felt like an eternity. No food. No water. No
bathroom. Just me, sitting in my own urine and dwelling on
my hunger. Wondering when my father would kill me."

I couldn't imagine a child version of Josh standing in a
chamber like the ones he had put me into so many other times.

"At last, he came to me. He stood in front of the chamber. I did not know what to expect."

Josh seemed to be immersed in the memory.

*"I could have never foreseen such a dreadful event," his father
said.*

"Father. I..." Josh held his hand out.

*"There are simply no words I need to hear from you right now,
Joshua." His eyes were red with exhaustion. Dark bags beneath them,
making him scarier than he was. "I have spent the last few weeks deciding your fate. Contemplating our next step. Your mother is sick with
grief. However, I could not help but surmise that this may be an unfore-
seen opportunity. See, as much as we kill Powers, sometimes they kill us.
That being said, you have an incomparable opportunity here. Being a
Hunter with powers gives you a chance to become the most powerful man
in the world. Do you understand the advantage this gives us, Joshua?"*

A young Josh nodded enthusiastically, this information spark-

ing a fire inside him.

"I am not going to kill you. For that, you should be grateful. However, you will now be trained in an entirely different manner. You will study harder, and you will learn more than any Power before you. If you at any point do not follow this plan, I will not hesitate to kill you. Do you understand?"

"Yes, father."

Josh looked at me, his eyes returning to the present. "Three weeks later, I killed my first Power," he reminisced. "My father was indeed pleased." He paused, a slight twitch at the corner of his mouth catching my attention. "He also decided it would be beneficial for me to understand the tests we put Powers through. That way I would have a more accurate understanding of what to do to them. He tortured me for a week every month for ten years. I will not lie, I did gain enormous insight." The look on his face didn't show anything but sadness. An emotion I didn't think possible for him. Then with the blink of an eye that emotion was gone.

12
HEY THERE

Senior year, oh what an eventful year it was. The very first day, David was on me. Bastard couldn't even wait till day two. But I had made a decision that summer and last year's status quo would not be continuing. I wanted a normal school experience, and what I had was anything but that. And I mean after all, what is the point of being in school when you're smarter than most of the teachers anyway?

"Annie! I've missed you." His voice made me cringe. He walked up behind me and put his arm over my shoulder. "Did I ever tell you that you are incredibly hot?"

"Get your hands off me, asshole."

"Woah ho ho! Touchy on the first day."

"I'm not dealing with your bullshit, David." He pushed me against the lockers and smelled my neck on his way to my ear. *Friggin' animal.*

"Did you forget that they still don't know, Annie?"

I had my hands on his arm. "Oh you didn't tell them? Well then, allow me." My hands lit up, singing his arm, and he pulled his arm away in shock. I lifted him up with one arm and pushed him against the wall putting my mouth to his ear. "How do you like that?" I blasted his stomach with a hit that could have killed an ordinary person and he sunk to the ground. He was pissed but he couldn't move. "Oh look, now they know. Tell your dad I said hey." I walked away like a winner but in my head I was cursing up a storm.

As I was walking away, I saw him. The most mesmerizing person I had ever seen. He was staring at me through the crowd of eyes, and I couldn't look away. His gaze pulled me so far in that the world slowed down—like slow motion movie scene kind of slow. It was strange because he wasn't fazed by what I had just done. Everyone else had backed away, but not him. *He must be new*, I thought. I smiled at him and he immediately smiled back. *Holy crap.* If I could ever melt into a puddle and become a crazy lovestruck fan girl, that would have been the time. Perfect smile, perfect teeth, perfectly styled hair. Just perfect. Seriously.

I made it to class, but hardly made it through. I needed to know who he was. I had never been so drawn to someone before.

I didn't see him through my first two periods but in third period he was there. He saw me and his face brightened. I raised my eyebrow and returned a smile. He saw me use my powers. I know he did. I sat down a few seats away to be discrete, but he moved over. I melted as he flashed a perfect smile again. His eyes up close were just, ahh! Gray with little speckles in them, and a blue ring around the center. He reached his hand out.

"Hey. I'm Matt. Matthew Lance. You are?"

"Annie Winters." I reached my hand out but instead of shaking it, he kissed it.

"It's a pleasure to meet you, Annie." Someone raised him correctly. Damn.

❄ ❄ ❄

Somehow, I got through class and through the day—not without a lot of effort I may add. We found each other after school ended.

"Well hey there, Annie."

"Hello, Matt." I was smiling like an idiot, all through a deep blush.

"I see you're a Power, huh?" I lost my smile and swallowed nervously.

"Yeah." He came closer to me and I watched a rose begin to appear in his hand.

"Me too." He was smiling as he gave me the rose. "See you tomorrow."

But all I could think was *oh no*. A wave of nervous heat ran through me, my surroundings becoming a blur and my vision tunneling on Matt walking away. Josh couldn't find out. He just couldn't. *He will kill him.*

I guess Matt looked back because he came back to me. Fast.

"Annie? Annie." I was dizzy with fear. "Sit down." He brought me to a bench but instead I grabbed his hand and pulled him into an empty classroom. I almost started crying I was so scared. I had known this kid for about two hours and already I was losing it. *Ya big baby.*

"Matt, listen closely. You can't tell anyone. No one. This isn't a very Power friendly place to be."

"Woah, woah. Okay. Relax. If we are being honest here, no place is very Power friendly."

"No but it's worse here. The Hunter here is just … just … please."

"I have dealt with Power Hunters before. They don't bother me." I couldn't take my eyes off of him.

"You don't understand. Have any of your Power Hunters had … powers?" He looked shocked by the question.

"No." He laughed, "That would be a bit contradictory. Don't you think?"

Yeah tell me about it, I thought. Meanwhile his luminous eyes were killing me. His perfectly styled brown hair, dear God! *Okay okay, back on track.*

"I know we just met, but you have to trust me. Josh Hunter is a ruthless man."

"Wait wait wait. *Josh* Hunter?" His voice had a sense of understanding, and fear, in it. Everyone knows who Josh is. "Okay. Okay."

I sighed, "Thank you. Thank you, Matthew."

13
WHO ARE YOU?

We spent a lot of time together that first week. He would walk me to class every day and then walk me home when the day was over. Emily and Miguel really seemed to like him, which meant the world to me.

"So, Matt, do you have any brothers or sisters?" Miguel asked, while eating an apple. Always the family man.

"Yeah. I have an older brother actually."

"Did he move here with you?" Miguel asked.

"He helped me with the move, but he's in the army so he isn't really home, ever."

"I give those guys credit. Really. Do you worry a lot?" Emily asked.

"I do. He's my brother, all I've got." But he smiled. "He is strong and a smart guy though. So I know he will be home."

"Where did you guys move from?" Emily wondered.

"The city."

"You left New York to come to Jersey?" Miguel was shocked.

"Yeah," he laughed. "There were some issues at home."

"Parents?" Miguel asked, sympathetically.

"Uh. No. My parents aren't in the picture."

"Oh. I'm sorry." Miguel was embarrassed.

"Hey man, it's alright." Despite the now saddened mood, Matt smiled. "What about you guys? Do you have siblings?"

"Well I don't. I'm on my own," Emily stated.

"I do," Miguel said as his cheeks returned to a normal color. "I have a little sister and brother."

"That's always fun. How old?"

"Gabriella is six and Diego is nine."

"Nice," Matt said, laughing. "You must adore them."

"Gabby is my favorite," Emily noted. "She is hilarious."

"Yeah she is a pistol that one," Miguel agreed and I nodded my agreement.

"Annie beats us though. Right, Ann?"

"I have three brothers and a sister," I volunteered. Not commenting on the fact that they were actually all my cousins.

"Wow! That's gotta be interesting." Matt responded.

"They are much older though. So I only really see them on some holidays. Nick is the only one still around here."

"How much older is he?"

"Six years."

"Does he live at home with you?"

"Sometimes. But most of the time he stays at his shop apartment," I said. "He owns a mechanic shop in town."

Matt smiled at me and his shining eyes made me melt yet again. I guess I didn't hide my reaction as well as I had thought, because Emily winked at me. I playfully rolled my eyes with a smile.

We finished our lunches, engaging in smatterings of small talk until the bell rang.

"Hey, Matt?" I said as we got up to head to class.

"Yeah. What's up?"

"I was wondering..." I paused nervously. "Would you like to hang out after school today?"

"Absolutely," he said without hesitation.

"Really?"

"Yeah," he laughed. "I'd love that."

"Okay. Perfect. Umm.... I'll meet you in front after school. Okay?"

"Can't wait." He gave me a hug and walked into his class. I breathed out dreamily and continued to mine.

The day, of course, took forever to finish. So, when it did, I sprinted outside where he was already waiting. I slowed down a bit; I didn't want to look *too* eager. He turned toward me and the sun made his eyes shine. Of course.

"I figured we should go to your house. Mine is full of boxes." Matt said casually.

I looked down. My Uncle was there. I had hoped to go to his but instead: "Of course!" I faked a smile, burying my concern. But he noticed.

"Hate to break it to you, but you're a terrible liar," he said, smiling.

"My uncl... my dad is kind of a jerk. I try to avoid him," I said scornfully.

"Then we'll go to my place—as long as you don't mind walking through my mess," he offered jokingly.

"I don't mind at all."

"I will admit there isn't much to do. Everything is packed," he said, still a bit uncertain.

"Oh please. It's fine. I want to get to know you. It doesn't matter." We walked slowly to his house, and each moment was filled with conversation. And leave it to me to start it out nice and easy.

"So if you don't mind me asking, did you guys move here because of your parents?"

"In a sense. My uh … my mom was very sick for most of my life. Cancer. My dad and brother, Joey, were always away. Dad was a general in the army and my brother is a first lieutenant. Big army family here. I was the one who took care of her. But this wasn't a battle we could win." He got quiet.

"Matt, I am so sorry. We don't have to talk about this. I shouldn't have brought it up."

"Nah, it's okay. If I'm going to talk about it to anyone, it's gonna be you." Heat flushed my face. "Two years ago, she finally passed. My brother and I were devastated, clearly, but almost happy. She was in so much pain that it was a gift for her to pass. My dad, on the other hand, was destroyed. The man could go through wars, but heartbreak … not so much. It literally killed him."

Man did I feel bad for bringing it up. He looked at me as we walked, my face full of apology and sympathy.

"It's okay. Really. Death is not something that bothers or scares me. Of course I miss them. I miss them every day," he looked at me, a crooked smile appearing on his face. "But I know they're together. Not broken or in pain. Just…" he breathed out a sigh of relief, "just happy. Looking down on Joey and me." He was as sure as can be. So effortlessly content. "That's why I try to live my best life. I know my mom is up there, and she would be damned if I didn't continue living through joy."

"I think you're the only person who could take a conversation like that and give it a happy ending."

He smiled, chuckling. "It's a gift. My mom used to call me a hopeless optimist. She wasn't wrong."

"Definitely not." I smiled back.

"Home sweet home," he scoffed as we walked up the stairs and through a screened porch into his home. He wasn't kidding, the house was full of packed boxes. But I couldn't have cared less. I just wanted to be with him. "It's small, but I like it," he said. "Here's my room." We sat down on his bed after he pushed all the boxes to the floor. I took a moment to gaze around the room. It was small, like he said. The walls were lined with worn blue wallpaper that was starting to tear off. The bed, being the only piece of furniture in the room, unless you count the boxes and paper, was actually made. Army style. It was a quite comedic scene.

"Yeah, it's a bit of a fixer upper. But hell, I have time," he said as he took a seat next to me. "My turn for a question. When did you get your powers?"

"When I was ten, actually."

"Ten? Woah! That's young. I got them at fourteen."

"I mean, that is young, too," I reminded him.

"Yeah, but ten? Usually the norm is fifteen. Were you alone?"

"No, I wasn't. Unfortunately."

"What happened?" he asked, concern filling his voice.

I sat in silence for a moment, biting my lip. He said sincerely, "You can tell me."

My eyebrow went up, an action that, by the way, it

tends to do all on its own. "It was at recess, fourth grade. So of course, everyone was there." I shook my head and rolled my eyes. "I was playing soccer with my friends and I stopped dead in my tracks. An unnatural warmth washed over me and my hands felt like they were burning. My legs went numb and I fell. When I looked at my hands, they were glowing. I couldn't understand why. What was happening? Was I dying? I… it didn't really process that I was getting them. You know?"

"I know exactly what you mean. What was everyone doing?" he asked gently.

"They all stepped away from me. Staring. In shock." Still sitting on Matt's bed, I looked down at my hands and sighed. "Probably thinking 'what a freak!' And it only got worse. My eyes started to glow. That's when everyone *really* started freaking out. Kids started screaming, teachers came running, but no one knew what to do."

"Talk about public announcements," he said, trying to lighten the mood.

"Yeah…. Well David Hunter was in school with me. He had never particularly liked me, but now a different hatred formed. I guess he thought he could save the day since it was his father's job, so he stepped forward. At this point I had lost control of my body; my powers had put me in defense mode."

"Oh God," Matt exhaled.

"David came toward me and my eyes snapped to him. My arms flew up, my hand opened and I cried as I felt the power grow in my fingers. Before I could shoot he knocked me down to the ground, but somehow he ripped my necklace off."

"That's bad?"

I laughed but no joy came to me. "Yeah. Yeah that's really bad. See my mom gave it to me and told me to always keep it on. I didn't know why, until that day. It's a filter meant to harness the extreme power I have. The maximum I can reach. Because it's evil."

"Evil?" he questioned, clearly not believing me.

"It's the only explanation I can come up with, because the power is so overwhelming that I practically lose myself to it," I said. "So when David ripped my necklace off, I was no longer myself. He tried to pin me down but he couldn't. I pushed him off me and put him in an extract hold."

"Wait, at ten you could do an extract hold?" Matt asked. He was impressed. The ability to perform an extract hold is extremely rare and risky business; only a few Powers can do it.

"Yup. I can when my necklace is off."

"That's incredible," he exclaimed.

"Not when you almost kill the son of a the most well-known Power Hunter. David didn't even have powers yet. I was ripping him apart from the inside out.

"I don't know who called him, but Josh showed up. I looked at him; he looked so familiar, but I didn't know why. Again, I was ten. Within two minutes he got my necklace back on me. I was exhausted," I said, fighting back tears. "He went over to David to make sure he was okay and then he picked me up and put me in his car. David sat in the front making sure I didn't leave and Josh told us to wait there. He held an assembly. With the whole school. I am one hundred percent sure he erased their memories, because from then on everyone continued about their days as if nothing more than a game of soccer had occurred. No powers involved. As far as they were concerned, I was a completely normal kid."

"Holy shit."

"Mhm. To this day I don't understand why he did it. Why make them forget? It's like he can't decide whether to kill me or let me live a normal life. Wouldn't it be easier for him if I was an outcast." I shrugged, "On the way to my house there was barely a word spoken. Josh spoke only to David. "I cannot comprehend the reasons for your actions, David. We will discuss this at length when I arrive home," I said, in my best Josh imitation. "He dropped David off at their home and made his way to mine."

By now, I was fully immersed in the memory. It was like it was happening all over again.

"Miss James, I have been waiting for this day for quite a long time now. I did not realize your necklace was a harness for some of your abilities, but now we know not to remove it. Do we not?"

"Wh … who are you?" I was floating in and out of consciousness.

"I am your biggest fan." He smiled at me —maniacally. "Do not worry. I will be gone for a few years before I deal with you."

"Please don't hurt me," I whimpered.

He laughed. "I will not do anything yet, my dear. Do not concern yourself with such trivial fears." He parked in front of my house and carried me to the front door. He rang the bell and Nick opened the door.

"Annie!"

"What happened?" my uncle asked with a grim tone. "Josh Hunter?" His eyes fell on me. "What did you do, you little bitch?"

"Brett, honestly," Heather warned.

"Mr. Winters, there was a situation today during school, which I handled. However, Annie did receive her powers today so she will need some rest," he stated calmly.

"My uncle locked me in my room and didn't let me step

outside or see anyone, for six years," I said, snapping myself back to the present. "He wasn't exactly a pleasant caretaker. Still isn't."

"Annie.... I can't believe that. That's ... that's ... I'm so sorry," Matt finally said.

"It's not your fault. That's why I didn't want to go to my house, though. I can't stand being around him."

"I don't blame you, and you can come here whenever you want. Anytime."

"Thank you, Matt." I blushed as he came in for a hug. He slowly pulled back from the hug and we looked at each other, both feeling the pull toward each other like magnets. Finally, his lips touched mine.

The world faded away. No troubles. No fear. No danger. It all felt obsolete when Matt kissed me. The only noise our breathing. I felt him as his hand brushed my cheek and ran through my hair. I wrapped my arms around his neck and let myself be lost, for once.

14
MY ANGEL

Matt and I started dating about one minute after that kiss. It just came to us naturally; I loved him more than I had thought possible. And I know what you're thinking, I was young and in love, aaah. Matt and I, we were different. Soul mates, hands down.

Luckily, we were able to keep the truth away from Josh, so he didn't bother Matt. He wasn't bothering me either. He hadn't abducted me in over a month. *What was he up to?* To tell you the truth, I was too happy to care.

However, I did come across a small challenge as you can imagine. The school wanted me out. The town called me to a meeting, the looks on their faces were not at all comforting. Fear. Disgust. Anger. We sat at a large table, me at one end, them all crowded together at the other. *For heaven's sake, what am I going to do? Spontaneously combust?* I thought.

"As you know, this county has a strict rule against Powers receiving schooling," started an old white man sitting at the very head of the table, definitely overemphasizing *strict*. "How you got in in the first place escapes us. We have received word from a large part of the community that you have publicly used your powers during an altercation. Do you deny this?"

"No. I don't." I said, matter of factly. Clearly, he had expected me to say yes. He was momentarily speechless.

"Very well," continued the woman sitting next to him. "In that case, we will be expelling you from school, effective as soon as we sign the forms. If you're found in or around the school, you will be detained immediately."

Why did I even try to go to school? "You realize I was there for a year without any detection. Why not let me just finish up this year?"

"Out of the question," the old man barked. "You are in direct violation of county and national laws. You are lucky we aren't sending you straight to Joshua Hunter."

There goes the eyebrow. "Fine. I am eighteen years old and smarter than your entire staff anyway."

And that ended that, as quick and abrupt as it seems. That's just how it went. *Guess I'm on permanent vacation.*

※ ※ ※

I was at home reading in my room when I heard, "Baby!" outside the window. I ran outside and jumped into Matt's arms, melting into him and his kiss. "I have a surprise for you." His smile was brilliant. Ear to ear. We walked behind my house and into the forest, him pulling me along like an excited dog, dragging its owner behind. We walked for quite a while, "Okay!" he said finally, stopping. He looked at me and exhaled excitedly. The smile never left his face, the excitement filling his eyes until they sparkled in the sun.

"Matt, my angel-face, I love you dearly and you know that," I said, putting my hand on his chest. "But I have been to the forest behind my house before so this isn't much of a surprise," I laughed.

"Smart ass." He pulled me to his chest and I leaned my head on his shoulder. That was my favorite. I had never felt as safe as I did when his arms were around me. His cologne flooded my senses and I could have just died happy right there.

"Okay, okay," he said. He let me go and looked at me. "I know you like to practice your powers and I figured I would make something for you. After all, you're an official adult now."

Matt is what we Powers call a "Traveler." That is a Power who, obviously, specializes in traveling. At certain ages they receive the ability to fly and speed run, or even just blink to where they want to be or go. They can also create portals. However you want to word it, it's pretty cool. I wouldn't mind being able to do that.

"I know you practice your abilities in the forest and that's not cool. So, I made this. What I need you to do is remember this spot, okay?"

"Alright. Right between the tree and the tree. Got it," I joked.

"Shush," Matt said. "Now hit this spot." So I lit up my hand and hit the ground with a power that would usually just move objects, but instead a portal opened. My eyes widened as I stared at the swirling light before me.

"Holy crap." I walked forward with Matt, his hand on my back. "Matt! This is incredible!" When we entered the portal, I was struck with amazement.

"Happy birthday, my angel." He built me my very own practice field in an old warehouse. There were rows of heavy bags, and dummies. Racks of swords and weaponry lined the walls. Against another wall sat a line of computers. Lights flashing and preparing different training regiments.

"It's perfect!" I jumped into his arms and he spun me around. "Where are we though?"

"Far. Like Saharan Desert far. No one will find it and it's all yours. The portal will be here forever. Unless you destroy it, of course. It is set to open for only you. Cool, huh?"

"It's amazing." I was so happy. I ran my hands through his hair. "Why are you perfect?"

He smiled and pulled me into his arms, kissing my forehead gently. He drew his face near to my ear and whispered. "Annie, for you, I'd do anything."

My body trembled feeling his soft lips against my face. Matt held me tighter than I had ever been held. His hands ran through my hair and somehow made their way down my back. I could feel his heartbeat begin to race as his hands slowly descended toward my hips. His breathing matched mine, shallow with short whimpers. Whimpers of longing for his hands to continue exploring my body.

I could not help myself. I was ready. Ready for him to see me at my most vulnerable; able to let my walls crumble. Ready for him to make me his and for me to make him mine. I wanted this, and apparently, my powers knew it too. Before I could contain myself, my hand lit up and waved to the side. Tiny particles scattered across the room, coming together to materialize a bed. I pulled my hand back to my mouth and let out a small giggle as I felt the cheeks on my face warm. I looked up, still wrapped in his arms and our eyes met. Those crystal eyes, piercing into mine. He had me, and he knew it.

He spun me around, settling me gently onto my back.

The cool cushion of the bed was no match for the radiating heat in my body. He slowly began to nuzzle my neck, one tender kiss at a time; his hand explored lower, just under my jeans, but he waited for some sort of approval that what he was doing was alright.

His eyes seemed to ask: Are you sure? I raised my eyebrow in return, a smile tugging at my lips. My eyes said: Just hurry up because I need you.

His hand slid down my pants and it was then that I felt his fingers inside me. I opened my mouth but no words could form. No sound could leave my lips. I felt as if I were paralyzed by his fingers. What power they held over me at that moment! Before I had met Matt, it felt like all I had experienced was pain. But this, what I was feeling now, was pure ecstasy. I was instantly addicted. He was so gentle and perfectly rough at the same time. I fell more in love with him with each touch.

He continued kissing my neck, each kiss a bit lower than the one before. Hovering only briefly on my breast I watched as he positioned his head between my legs, pulling my pants the rest of the way down. The heat coursing through me became impossible to contain. My arms scrambled above my head trying to find something to grab onto to keep my body still. I grabbed the sheets pulling them toward me to prevent my legs from shaking. As my head sprung up from the mattress, strands of light escaped from my fingertips through the sheets and onto the floor like roots from a tree.

❖ ❖ ❖

I awoke the next morning to the sunlight blanketing the old warehouse. I looked around to see Matt moving gracefully in the rays of sun, barefoot and shirtless on a large excercise mat.

Slowly, I untangled myself from the sheets and walked quietly behind him. "It's beautiful," I said softly.

"Like you," he said, continuing the motions. "It's called form. My brother and I grew up training in different forms of martial arts." He moved his arms slowly in sync with his legs. "My father wanted us to be prepared for any possible dangers. I believe that without control of your body and mind, there's no control of your powers." He finished his form and I wrapped my arms around his bare chest.

"Could you teach me?"

"You want to learn form?"

"I want to learn how to fight. How to defend myself. I am tired of just *getting by*. I want to be able to fight."

"You aren't a fighter."

"No, I'm not a *killer*. There's a difference."

"Hmm, this is true," he said thoughtfully. "How about this," he spun me around softly wrapping his arms around mine. "We start with tai chi. You get a basis of balance and technique, then I teach you to fight."

"Fair enough," I exhaled, letting him spread my arms out.

"Want your first lesson?"

I smiled in return.

15
GOOD TO SEE YOU

A month after this perfect day, Josh returned from his hiatus. He didn't waste a second in coming to see me either. But since I didn't know he was back, I was with Matt at the time. It was the biggest mistake of my life.

Matt and I were walking home from the movies late one night when I felt the P.T. shots pierce my skin. I started falling almost immediately.

"Annie! Annie, baby? What's wrong?"

"Run," I tried to tell him but all my strength was gone. I couldn't move but I wasn't blacking out. *Why?*

"Annie!" Matt picked me up and that's when Josh came. He wanted me to *watch* Matt get caught. Some guys grabbed me while others grabbed Matt. I still didn't think they knew he was a Power. Then Josh came out; it was weird seeing him do his own work for once. As they carried me into the van, Josh walked up to Matt who asked, "Who the fuck are you?"

Then Josh shot him, with a regular gun.

They carried Matt into the van and Josh sat next to me. "Miss James, I have missed you immensely. Still, I had an exceptional trip. Did you know there are more Powers on the West Coast than any other place in the United States? Not as many now, but you can thank me later."

I'm not sure if I mentioned this, but did you know I hate him?

"I leave ever so briefly and you get yourself a boyfriend?" he continued. "I do not approve but I will let it slide this time. And a Power nonetheless! Well done."

How the hell does he know? Maybe David found out and told him. Maybe we weren't careful enough.

"It is so nice talking to you when you are quiet. Mildly less entertaining, however." He stared at me and I cringed. "It is quite astonishing how much you resemble your mother. Those eyes," he said. My inability to respond was sucking the amusement for him from the encounter. "We will talk more later."

When we arrived, Josh put Matt and me in separate, yet adjacent, chambers. He didn't strap me down this time; I guess he had all the tests he needed. Matt, on the other hand, wasn't tied down either. *What is Josh up to?*

As Matt started to wake up he looked up and saw me. *My poor baby.*

"Annie. What the hell is going on?" he asked groggily, looking around at our surroundings.

"Remember when I told you about Josh?" He nodded. I raised my hands as if to say well, here we are.

"Well, hell," he said, as Josh walked in. I will admit, the man always had perfect timing.

"Well, hello, young lovebirds. Miss James and Mr. Lance. What an endearing couple," he drolled on.

"Josh, you let him go, you son of a bitch," I growled.

"Let me ask you something, Annie. Why do you think I would go through the trouble of bringing you both here to merely let you go?"

"Fuck you," I replied with acid in my tone.

"Every time you show complete and utter disrespect today, Mr. Lance will receive the consequence for your action."

"No!" I banged on the chamber and then looked at Matt. "I'm so sorry, baby," I cried as Josh activated his chamber. Matt's screams ran through me like ice water.

"Josh, stop!" I was on my knees. It physically hurt to watch this. Each shock sent through Matt, vibrated through my bones as well. "NO!"

"The intensity of the punishment will only increase if you continue to argue." Josh increased the voltage; Matt's screams pierced my ears. I started to cry while Josh stood there, smiling. There were so many things I wanted to say to him but couldn't say any of them.

"You're a piece of shit," Matt said as the electricity stopped. *Oh no, Matt.*

"You have anything further to add, Miss James?" I shook my head. "Good. Now I heard you are a Traveler, Mr. Lance. Is this true?"

"Yeah it's true. I'll drop you with the fucking sharks," Matt threatened.

"What a gentleman you have found," Josh said unaffectedly.

I wanted to kill him.

"Talk time is over, little lovers. Work time." The table

slid out of an opening in the bottom of the chamber. Then the wires slithered out and grabbed onto Matt pinning him against the table. I then watched as Josh searched for his pressure points like he had done to me. I could see Matt trying to travel out of it, but he was glitching. He would flash in and out of view like a broken video game.

The laser lights of the bracelets went into his palms and he screamed louder. Then the chamber I was in started to fill with gas. I assumed it was my P.T., just aerosolized.

"Matt, I'm sorry, baby! I'll get you out."

16

SHE HULK

"Well hello, gorgeous."

"Hi, handsome."

"How is your weekend going?"

"Been stuck at home but it is pretty good now." I smiled. "How about yours?"

"It's alright and I must agree. It's much better now. I've been thinking about you every day."

"Spending all your free time thinking about me," I said sarcastically. "And what about me has you so hung up? Hmm?"

"Everything. Your radiant smile, your golden hair, your ocean blue eyes." We were walking to town. He went for my hand and I couldn't resist. His grip was so strong and he was so warm.

He stared into my soul with his beautiful eyes. Matt was the kind of person who just understood. He loved people but could also stand up for himself, much like me. He didn't let anything bother him though. Nothing could get him down. Life was a playground to him.

"Are you ready?" Matt asked.

"Why yes, I am."

"So then where would you like to go tonight? New York? Rome? Paris?"

"Rome. Definitely Rome." I smiled with excitement.

"Alright. Hold onto me." I wrapped my arms around him and we started to travel.

❀ ❀ ❀

I woke up from the dream of our first date, not even a month ago, to remember where I *really* was.

"Baby?" I said, panicked.

"Ann, I am right here," he responded from the chamber next to me, his voice sounded tired.

"Shit," I said, rolling over to face him. I put my hands against the chamber wall. "I will get us out of here. Where is Josh?"

"He has been gone for hours. At least it feels like hours."

I scanned the room. No guards. Probably outside in the hallway. Or slacking off somewhere while the boss is gone. Good.

I pressed both hands against the glass in front of me. I took the utter fear and anxiety weighing on my chest and focused it all into my hands. While practicing in the forest one day, many summers ago, I had made an object explode with my touch. At the time, it seemed quite useless. But now... maybe with a little bit of luck, and pure concentration, I could get this chamber to explode around me. *Worth a try.*

With my hands against the chamber wall I closed my eyes. I tried connecting with the glass, sensing the particles making it solid, the fibers making it power resistant. I pushed my power through those fibers. Fitting in between them, filling

81

the space with pure energy, the effort making me light-headed. I opened my eyes to see the entire wall glowing.

"Woah," Matt commented.

Agreed, baby. Then I let go. And with that, the glass completely shattered. I was in awe. It worked! And it was loud. *Speed it up, Annie.*

Using the screen in front of Matt's chamber, I let him out. I guess they didn't think we would ever be on the other side so there weren't any codes to decipher. One good thing.

Then the guards came running in, guns blazing. I looked at Matt and released his power restraints from him. His eyes glowed and his powers returned. So I looked at the guards.

"Too late, fellas," I said as Matt and I traveled to anywhere but there with a rush of wind at our exit.

"Holy hell," Matt exclaimed.

"I agree," I responded as we gained our footing. "Are you okay?"

"Could be worse. That man is insane. Can I just say?"

"Matthew," I glared at him. Eyebrow raised.

"Yeah, I'm okay." He brought us to his house. "I'm sorry. I didn't have much energy in me to go further."

"Don't you dare apologize. This is on me, handsome."

"It absolutely isn't. *You* didn't put me in that chamber. *You* didn't send electricity through me. *You* got me out."

"Bu..."

"Uh-uh. Let's get out of here first." He pulled me tightly into his chest. I closed my eyes. We traveled again, the feeling of being on a roller coaster becoming oddly comforting.

It was dark when we emerged at his destination, seconds later.

"Where did you bring us this time?"

"Iceland, where the grass is green."

His humor, normally charming, was not really helpful this time. My anxiety was more rampant than ever.

We walked down the streets of Reykjavik until we found a nice, unassuming hotel.

"We will figure this out, baby," he comforted as we sat down on the small bed. "I have enough money for the next few weeks and then I can hack my way into the hotel systems."

"I'm not worried about the money, Matt."

"I know that," he said looking down at his hands. He got off the bed and kneeled in front of me. "I will run with you until the end of my days."

"Poor choice of words, jerk."

"Josh isn't going to kill me. It ain't happening."

"I couldn't handle it if he did."

"I am staying right here."

"I am so in love with you."

"And I am more in love with you." He smiled his big goofy smile and brought me right into his playful, no-worry world again.

❀ ❀ ❀

After an incredibly restful and wonderfully refreshing night's sleep, we woke up and started walking the streets. We eventually rented a car, we had fake ID's. Hey, I never said I was an angel. We made the most of our location, and started traveling along the roads wrapped in endless beauty. The rolling green hills brought an indescribable calm over me. Everything so fresh. Untouched, almost.

Every place we went was enthralling to Matt. It was as if every place we went was his favorite. Everything was excit-

83

ing and new. His smile, brilliant and beautiful. I watched every reaction. I mean, I guess I should have been looking at the blue of the glaciers or the white capping the mountaintops, but he was a view in and of himself.

We found a small hiking path and made our way up. Surprisingly, no one else was there. So once we got to an open area we decided it would be a missed opportunity if we didn't do some martial arts work. Yes, we are *that* couple.

Now I am going to assume you've never trained with a Traveler before, so let me fill you in. It's hard work.

They don't stand still. It's really helpful, don't get me wrong. He decked me in the face one too many times. Mostly because he'd be in front of me one second and behind me the next. It was like fighting ten people instead of one.

Helpful. Yes. Frustrating. Yup! But man did I learn.

17
CATCH ME IF YOU CAN

Moments with Matt seemed to speed by. Not in the sense that time was rushed, but as if the old saying "time flies when you're having fun" were true. Matt and I started to country hop. For the record, I wanted to contact Nick and tell him I was okay, but the fear of being recaptured or putting him in danger held me back. Every new place we landed was a mystery to us. We explored together, laughed together, and, most importantly, we created memories together. In just a little over two weeks I had mastered just about all the tai chi he had taught me. Information retention, remember? Learning tai chi gave me the chance to release my thoughts and relax my mind in a way I had never really gotten the chance to do before. It was one of the most comforting things I had ever experienced taught to me by the man I loved most. What more can a girl ask for, right?

We moved to tae kwon do and jiu jitsu. I trained harder

than I ever have in my life. I finally started feeling like a competent fighter. Matt was right too, the control over my body strengthened the connection to my powers—a very welcomed bonus. But no matter how much training we completed together, we had to keep ourselves on high alert. Making sure Josh stayed far off our trail was, of course, our biggest goal. However, no matter where we traveled, we kept seeing men who worked for Josh. They weren't trying to capture us. They were just watching.

Matt and I were sitting together on a remote beach in Bermuda watching the waves smash into the sandy pink beach when a thought bolted through my mind.

I sat up straight, annoyed with my own stupidity.

"Trackers."

"Huh?" he said, still laying back with his sunglasses on.

"We have to be tagged. I mean out of everything he did to us, there is no way he wouldn't ensure we could be found."

"Oh ... duh."

"Yeah I know. So dumb. Why in God's name did it take me this long to think of it?" For someone so smart, I sure am slow. I mean we had just been getting frustrated and moving instead of finding a solution.

"You can't think of everything all the time, baby. So don't go beating yourself up." *Too late.*

Other than rapid healing and enhanced hearing, some Powers also have X-ray vision. The trifecta of usefulness.

"Stand up," I said to Matt.

"Okay," he responded, taking off his sunglasses.

I concentrated on him and slowly my eyes scanned through his clothes and then layers of skin and muscle. Finally I could see his organs, moving with the rythm of his breathing.

Then I saw it. A small pill shaped object. It seemed to have veins coming out of it, attaching to whatever surrounded it.

"Oh boy."

"What is it?"

"It's definitely what has been tracking us. But it has somehow organically attached itself to the surrounding organs."

"Yum."

I shot him a look.

"If this has been here through all the torture he has put us through, it has to have resistance to electric currents."

"So I guess this means you don't secretly have surgery experience, huh?"

I gave him another look. "No I can't say I do. Miguel's dad clearly will."

A slight flash of fear crossed Matt's face.

"I know. Going back to town isn't ideal. But if we can get in and out quickly, Josh won't have time to take us in."

"You think Miguel's dad can work that fast?"

"Well we don't exactly need the same preparation humans do. We don't have to worry about infections, so we don't need a sterile environment. We don't need anesthesia, our pain tolerance is higher. We don't need stitches to close anything, because we will heal quickly. We..."

"Okay, baby. Those are all incredibly valid points. But don't you think this is basically handing ourselves over?"

I stopped to think. We *would* be dangerously close to Josh's building.

"Let's travel then. Maybe Miguel's dad would be okay traveling with us to be safe. It's worth a shot. I don't know the first thing about surgery. If we tried cutting each other open we would end up causing more pain than necessary."

"Alright. I trust you. Let's give it a shot."

We walked back to our hotel, and traveled from our room.

I knocked on the front door of Miguel's house and he answered. Man it was nice to see his face.

"Holy shit, Annie!" He pulled me into a hug.

"Annie's here?" I heard Emily ask from the other room. She came to the door.

"Thank God," she said, pulling me into an even bigger hug than Miguel had just given.

"Hey guys," we walked in. "I am so sorry I never texted you or anything. I really am. We ditched our phones early on."

"Oh who cares about that. Are you guys okay?" Em asked.

"Yeah. We just had to escape for a while. Needed to get a break from this town. We thought our phones would be too easily tracked but it turns out that we are actually tagged."

"What?" Emily exclaimed.

"Josh has us tagged with trackers, internally, so we are actually looking for your dad," Matt explained.

"And we probably don't have much time," I added.

"Fuck, uh, I think he is at the clinic today. Let me call him." Mig whipped out his phone and stepped away.

"Not gonna lie, I was beginning to get really nervous," Emily said.

"I really am sorry."

"I know you are, sweetie, and it's not your fault. I don't blame you for coming out. You were getting the shit beat out of you every day. I would have left too if I were you. I'm just glad you're not alone," she said, looking to Matt.

"Not for a second," Matt confirmed.

"Alright, so Dad is at the clinic. He said you can go there right now, he is making himself available," Mig said, re-entering the room.

"Amazing. I can't thank you enough, Mig," I said.

"You are more than welcome, now go."

"Please be careful, and update us when you can," Emily interjected.

"I will." We did a quick round of hugs and booked it to the clinic.

❖ ❖ ❖

We traveled to a spot right behind the clinic and then walked around to the entrance and straight to his office.

"Dr. Alvarez, we can't thank you enough so for letting us come in."

"You already know it is no problem. Miguel mentioned trackers?"

"Yeah, the trackers Josh implanted in us have attached themselves to our organs. Long story short, we need them out and you are the only person we could think of to go to."

"But we would have to travel somewhere farther and safer," Matt said.

"Bueno. Let me grab some supplies and I will be ready."

"He's serious? No questions asked?" Matt asked me incredulously.

"He's an incredible man," I said.

"What is it?" Matt asked, looking at me. He could see the resignation and frustration in my face.

"You wouldn't be in this mess if you hadn't met me."

"Don't start, baby. Because I also wouldn't be as happy. Or smile as much. I wouldn't have had the chance to see that smile of yours, or hear your laugh. I wouldn't have had the chance to know your heart. And that is a beautiful thing."

You can bet I was blushing.

"But I know you are scared, and it's my fault."

"Alright so I am a little scared. It's Josh Hunter, he's freaking scary. But how do you know he wouldn't have found me without you here? I'm a Power with or without you around. So will you please cut yourself some slack for once?"

"Probably not."

"Just try. For me," he flashed a huge smile. "Paleeee-ase?"

"Yeah yeah yeah. Okay."

He leaned over and kissed me.

"We are going to figure this all out. And then it's just you and me. We have the whole world to see."

"Bueno, niños." Dr. Alvarez walked in. "I am ready when you are."

Matt grabbed onto both of us and we quickly traveled back to our room in Bermuda.

"Oh..." Dr. Alvarez said, gaining his footing. "That is something I have never experienced."

"Sorry," Matt said, realizing he had given no warning. "I am so used to everyone having traveled before. My bad, sir. You okay?"

"All good. All good. Where are we?"

"Bermuda."

"Wow, I haven't been here in years. Anyway, let's get this going, huh?"

"We will lie right down on the beds. You don't have to worry about the environment," I told him.

"I figured, but I brought gloves and cleaning supplies

anyway. Where are the trackers?"

"They are lodged between the heart and the lungs."

"If that is the case, I may have to cut part of the breast-bone."

"Ow that does not sound fun," Matt commented.

"I brought a lot of sedation and numbing topicals for you both. I had a feeling this may get rough. Nothing is easy regarding Hunters."

"You do what you have to do, Dr. Alvarez."

"I am about to cut you open and you still call me Dr. Alvarez," he teased, trying to lighten the mood.

"Old habits?"

He just smiled. "Okay muñeca, you lay down and I will numb that area."

This was not my usual. So it was safe to say I was just a tad nervous. But I knew if there was anyone I could trust with my safety, this man was one of them. He said so himself when we met the first time.

"Just breathe. I will make it as quick and painless as possible. Can you tell me exactly where to start?" I pointed to a place on my chest and he nodded.

Whatever he used was strong, because I didn't feel a thing when he started. He did have to cut through part of my breastbone, as he had said, but all I felt was a large amount of pressure. No pain. Thank God we asked him.

"You weren't kidding when you said it attached itself. It has veins of its own to attach to your heart. I honestly don't know what will happen when I cut them. Are you ready?"

"As ready as I'll ever be, Doc."

He cut it and that is when I finally felt pain. I felt like I was having a heart attack.

"Oh fuck," I said.

"The veins are grabbing on tighter," Miguel's dad responded.

"Just keep going. You have to keep going."

Matt, who was already holding my hand through it, squeezed tighter.

"I am going to do one long incision across every vein. This will probably cause a lot of pain."

"Do it."

Well he did and holy dear God it hurt. But then Dr. Alvarez held the tracker in front of me so I could see it. The veins hung from the metallic casing.

"Done," he pulled out a hammer. "You have to go back to the basics sometimes," he commented when Matt gave him a questioning look. Then he put the tracker on the ground and smashed it with the hammer. "One down."

"That kind of super fucking sucked," I grunted.

"Let me stitch you up."

"That's not nec..."

"Annie, I know you heal. But as a doctor I can't allow myself to have you sit here with an open chest. Literally."

So of course I let him stitch me up. Then we both looked at Matt.

"Your turn, bud," I said to him.

"Ugh," Matt grumbled.

We went through the same thing for Matt. The tracker reacted the same way, and like I said, I am so happy we asked a doctor to do this. Because honestly, I don't think I could have stomached doing it ourselves. Let alone even knowing what to do!

Once he finished and stitched Matt up as well, we

thanked him profusely.

"I really hope some day we can repay you."

"Not necessary. Repay me by being safe. You are free now. Enjoy yourselves."

"Deal," I responded.

"Let me bring the good doctor home before Josh realizes what's going on."

"Good idea."

"Can you travel right after surgery?" Miguel's dad asked, concerned.

"Yes sir," he smiled. "I can do anything!" Back to jokes with this one.

"Thank you again. I'll see you around, *Enrique*." I flashed a smile of my own.

Then they traveled.

18

HEAT

"How about Paris?"

"Paris?"

Before I could finish responding we were traveling.

"It's the city of romance, my love!" he said in an exaggerated French accent. I laughed at him and made my way toward the window. It had been a few days since the trackers were removed. Now, we were on the top floor of a hotel and had a breathtaking suite. The doors opened to a patio with a perfect view of the Eiffel Tower. The suite was as extravagant as anything I had ever seen, my eyes darting from each perfectly decorated part of the room. The stairs wound their way up to a second level of the suite and I walked out onto the patio. I couldn't take my eyes off the city. I was in a trance, soaking in every light that sparkled across the streets of Paris, and it took a few seconds to register where Matt was.

"Don't you think?" he whispered. Startled by the sound

of his voice I came back to reality. *Ah, there he is.* My Matt with me in the most romantic city in the world. I let out a sigh and leaned my head back on his chest as his arms wrapped around me. This was my favorite way to stand with him, I felt safe. Leaning into him, having him hold me, gave me this feeling of stability. He was a part of me and I was a part of him. We had spent so much time together running, being hunted and always on constant alert, but for this second in time we were safe. For this second in time, as I leaned my body into his, his arms wrapped tightly around me, time had finally stopped.

Maybe it was the shimmering lights of the city below us, or perhaps it was the gentle kisses to my neck, but before I could realize it he had one hand on my chest and the other in my pants. I leaned back into him, sliding my hand down his pants. "Yes, I do." He started to moan but removed my hand from his body, picked me up, and put me on the bed. He unbuckled his pants and ripped them off; I did the same. I pulled him closer and he slowly pushed himself inside me. I screamed with pleasure and my arms slammed down on the bed as I grabbed the sheets. "Oh my God, Matt!"

He was moaning as he kissed my neck. I ran my hands along his back, scratching it as I moved down. He screamed out and I grabbed his hair, pulling him closer. We moved together rhythmically, becoming one. He went faster and harder and I couldn't hold it in. I moaned louder and louder with each push. I could not stop. I wanted more of him. My hunger growing. Just as I could feel Matt's body tense up, a knock hit the wood of the door.

"Bonjour? Qui est lá? Who is in there?" I looked at the door and flipped my hand at it making sure both locks were secure so no one could come in. I guess we were being just a bit too loud. Whoops.

I fell to the side and watched him, both of us breathing heavily. An hour later for all I know, maybe more. We just lay there, basking, cuddling, kissing. For once, utterly relaxed.

"You are amazing," I cooed.

"Yeah?" he asked. I nodded. "Annie? I love you." I sat up a little.

"Really?"

"Yeah. More than you could ever know." *How could I be so lucky? It's amazing how happy he makes me.*

19
NO EVER LOVING WAY ...

We spent another month in Paris exploring, tackling the tourist sites first, of course. The Eiffel Tower and Louvre Museum were our first two. The enormity of some of the paintings in the Louvre took my breath away. We took an amazing tour of Gustave Eiffel's private apartment and revisited later that night, traveling via Matt's powers. It was spectacular.

Then we made our way to the Bateaux Parisiens pier and took the infamous river tour on the Seine. I loved leaning up against Matt, his arm wrapped lovingly around me as he took in the views around him with excited light in his eyes.

He brought me everywhere: Notre Dame, the Tuileries Garden, the Basilica, Champ De Mars, the Catacombs—not my favorite—and the Ballon Generali. My favorite might have been the mountain in the Parc des Buttes-Chaumont. Something about it was incredibly alluring to me.

Matt had been using his incredible computer skills to

continue reserving the gorgeous suite for us without payment. Don't ask me how. As much as I know, I am not computer savvy. Either way, we figured it was probably getting a little suspicious at this point, which prompted our mutual decision to return home and make sure Josh wasn't wreaking havoc on our town.

But we didn't get the chance to go back home—at least not of our own volition.

Knock! Knock!

Matt and I looked at each other.

"Did you order anything?" I asked.

"No," he said, shrugging.

I tried to look through the door with X-ray vision, but it wouldn't work—not a good sign. I looked at Matt seriously, indicating he should prepare himself.

"Wait, Annie, something is wrong," Matt began, but it was too late. I had opened the door.

There in all her unparalleled beauty stood Ursula Hunter. We both shot at her, but it was futile. Our blasts turned into nothing but sizzling sparks in front of her and she pushed me effortlessly back onto the bed with her powers. Immediately I felt like my arms and legs had been coated in concrete. I could not move.

To top it all off, the window light on the walls of the room began to shimmer with an almost invisible force field. Clearly, Matt would be unable to travel.... It seemed Matt was in the same predicament as I was.

"Hello, love," she smiled at me, her mesmerizing eyes locking with mine. I said nothing but stared back resolutely. She turned around and started picking up our belongings one by one, nonchalantly examining them. "My husband is unhappy, Annie," she continued. "He has been incredibly worried about you." *Yes I'm sure worried is the word.* She glanced at me momentarily, eyebrows raised, as if she could hear my thought. She then returned to examining the room. "Don't worry yourself though. Luckily I have a rather large base right outside of France and caught you on surveillance yesterday."

Matt and I still could not move. We were both rigid on the bed.

"You're a little young to be this far from home. No?"

I finally grew the nerve to speak, "I am eighteen and I have no home."

"Hmm, yes, I understand what you mean. Home is a relative term. Nevertheless, I will take you back."

"I am bothering neither of you," I said with annoyance. "Why can't I be left alone?"

"Joshua is stubborn. Once he begins a job he will see it through until the end." She leaned up close to my face and crooned, "threat or not." She then turned to Matt; I tensed but it had no effect.

Her eyes narrowed as she scrutinized the details of his face. She then placed her hands on either side of his head. Closing her eyes, she tilted her head back as if letting warm water rush over her. A slight glow emanated from her hands.

"Decent amount of power," she said after a few moments. "What a shame."

"Shame?" I exclaimed. Her eyes landed back on me.

"Let's go!" She placed a hand on my shoulder and a hand on Matt's and within two seconds we were standing in Josh's all-too-familiar lab. "Honey, I'm home!"

Josh sat uncharacteristically slumped in the big black chair in front of his computer screens, his head resting on his hand. I could see DNA readings across the screen and a bunch of sequences with big red X's through them. But before I could look further the screens went black and he swiveled around.

"Ursula?" He stood up, running a hand through his disheveled hair and grabbed his suit jacket, swinging it over his shoulders and through his arms. It was then that he realized Matt and I were there. A smile spread across his face. "What a gift! Oh my love." He kissed her. She finally released her hold and Matt and I fell clumsily until we regained our footing. Josh's eyes drifted slowly to me. I stepped in front of Matt, who reached forward and rested his hand on the small of my back. She still had our powers dampened.

Josh was wearing a smile that made chills run through to my core.

So many obscenities were building in my head. But with *her* standing there I didn't want to risk them coming out of my big fat mouth so I held my lips tight.

"I have a homecoming gift for you," Josh said, a sense of excitement in his voice.

"Thanks, but I am going to politely decline." I pushed myself closer into Matt's chest.

"It is never polite to refuse a gift," Josh responded.

I glanced quickly at Ursula. She had wandered over to Josh's computers and reopened the files he had been working on when we entered. There in big bold letters on the top of the screen: "JAMES, ANNIE." A wave of nervous heat ran through me. Josh noticed.

"Yes. You are quite the conundrum. Your DNA profile is incredibly complex. *His* on the other hand, not so much," said Josh, nodding his head toward Matt without taking his eyes off of me.

"Excuse me?" Matt finally found his voice. Out of fear.

"Your DNA sequence w. . . "

"Absolutely not," I cut in with deep anger in my voice. I could feel my powers were still dampened but I fought against her hold as hard as I could. "Don't you dare." Sparks began to crack at my finger tips and Ursula turned around.

"How are you possibly fighting me?" She stepped toward me, her face full of curiosity not anger. "How exciting!" She approached me unnaturally quickly and grabbed my head as she had done to Matt. My own hands grabbed at her wrists, trying to loosen her grip, but she didn't budge. Suddenly I couldn't keep my eyes open and my legs became Jello and collapsed beneath me. A heat washed over my body and a pressure built within me. Just before I felt the darkness take over she released me and my powers rushed back. I'm not sure how long she had me there. Although it only felt like a second, it was long enough for a struggle between Matt and Josh to finish, ending with Josh holding Matt by the neck.

"You're like an overcharged battery!" Everything else Ursula said faded when I noticed the needle Josh held to Matt's neck. My breathing quickened.

"Welcome home, Miss James." Josh said as the needle went in, the contents irreversibly entering into Matt's system. His face contorted into utter pain.

It felt as if somebody had punched me in the gut and slapped me in the face all at once. All ability to breathe just left me. Josh dropped Matt to the ground. I walked to my love on numb legs and landed hard on my knees next to him. His body spasmed as light shot from his hands, his eyes emitting a light of their own. I picked him up into my arms, holding him tight to lessen the movement.

"Okay.... Okay baby. I'm here." He struggled in my arms, his powers leaving him for another agonizing minute. Finally, he went rigid and fell heavy into my lap. "Matt?" I held his face in one hand. "Matt.... Oh, God." The tears began to run down my face. Then he awoke with a deep breath, his eyes fluttering open. They were bloodshot from the stress of the loss. He didn't speak at first, his eyes speaking for him. Fear. Pain. Sorrow.

"I am sorry.... I..." My voice broke with sorrow of my own. Matt simply shook his head.

"N... not on you." He lifted his hand and tangled his fingers in my hair.

"I can't do this without you. I can't." My tears were now completely uncontrollable.

"Yes. You absolutely can." He pushed himself up to kneel in front of me, struggling to find the strength. Then hands grabbed him away from me and I snapped back to the reality of where we were. The guards lifted him up by his arms and began to drag him away.

"NO!" The scream was blood curdling and it came from my own mouth. I couldn't get up, so I whipped my head to Ursula and her eyes were locked on me. The slightest smile tugging at her lips. "Let me go!" Josh stepped up to Matt. "Stop, Josh.... Ursula, let me go!" I fought against her hold but it was like pushing against a wall. "Please," I begged with pure desperation.

"You belong to me, Miss James," he stated, with a punch to Matt's face. I closed my eyes as he landed another punch. A gun materialized in his hand.

"God no!" Matt met my gaze, his eyes still holding his life behind them.

"It's okay," I saw him mouth. "I love you, always."

"I love you t..."

Bang! My screams echoed with the gunshot as Matt fell lifeless to the floor. Ursula's hold on me broke and I scrambled to him and picked him up one last time. I cried onto his lifeless corpse for what felt like hours.

"I don't understand," I said softly. "You took my parents already. Why, for God's sake, did you have to take him too?"

"I need a reason?" Josh responded coldly.

"Let me bury him.... If you actually have any respect at all, let me bring him home and bury him." I looked up at Josh, his face unreadable. "Don't talk about respect if you can't show it yourself." I forced strength into my voice, feigning confidence.

He stared at me, lips tight. He then glanced down at Matt in my arms before his gaze finally landed on Ursula. Surprisingly enough, she nodded ever so slightly. Josh sighed and looked at me.

"Very well, Annie." He walked back to his computers leaving me alone with the love of my life in my arms.

❁ ❁ ❁

I was so lost. So stuck. I walked out of Josh's carrying Matt in both arms. The only thing I could think of was Nick. *Where would he be? His shop? The house?* It was night, the darkness accentuating the darkness taking me over.

Honestly, I don't remember the walk to Nick's shop or his apartment above it. I just remember him opening the door and trying to get my attention.

"Annie?" By the tone of his voice, it must have been the tenth time he had said my name.

103

"Huh," my focus came back and I saw his face with clarity. He had placed Matt on his couch inside yet I still stood in the doorframe of the small apartment.

"Annie, come inside." He placed his hand lightly on my shoulder. "Can you hear me?" I nodded and walked dazedly forward. "What happened?" I looked down at my hands. His blood.

"Josh..." my resolve was diminishing. "Found Matt's Formu... let me bring him... funera... I..."

He pulled me into his chest and I cried.

20
HELP ME FALL

When I woke the next morning covered in blankets in Nick's bed, the world couldn't have felt heavier. It was like waking up from a bad dream, except that a bad dream would be better than my reality. I screamed into the pillow with absolute frustration.

I pushed myself up and walked to the shower, dragging my feet behind me. Slowly stripping off my clothes, I stepped in. Every moment seemed to drag along. Finally, I turned the shower handle, letting the cool water run over my body until it turned warm.

I looked down at my hands one last time before washing off Matt's blood, the water already turning red at my feet. I scrubbed until my hands were raw, then leaned against the wall and sank down to the floor. I hugged my knees close and cried again. If given the chance I probably could have stayed there forever but a light knock came on the bathroom door.

"Annie?" It was Emily. "I put a new set of clothes on the bed for you." Her voice was soft, gentle. I didn't respond.

A long time later, I finally got out of the shower and wrapped a big towel around myself, then stared hard and long at myself in the mirror, wondering how in the world I got this life handed to me.

My clothes were laid out on the bed. Nice comfy sweatpants and a T-shirt. *Thanks, Em,* I thought.

When I walked out, Matt was no longer on the couch as I had remembered last night. My heart lurched. I took a deep shaky breath in and was about to ask where he was when Nick stepped gently forward, his hands open as if trying to calm someone.

"I had to go to the police, sis. I couldn't leave him here." It happened in an instant. One second I was five feet away from him, the next my hand was wrapped around his throat, his toes just skimming floor. His hands grasped at my wrist. My vision blurred.

"Anni..." he gasped out. "It's ... me."

"Annie," Miguel said, stepping forward. "That's Nick," he said in a calm yet urgent tone.

Slowly my vision cleared and I lowered Nick to the ground.

"I'm..." I looked at my hands as if they were a monster's claws.

"It's okay. I am okay," Nick stated. "See?"

My breathing quickened, and I kept shaking my head.

"Sit down." Emily cautiously walked over to me and rested her hands on my shoulders. She guided me to the couch and I sat down slowly.

"What's being done?" I managed to get out.

"I called Matt's brother, Joseph, last night. He is shipping out for his next tour in four days but he is coming here to set up the funeral first."

"What can I do?"

"Nothing," Emily responded.

"Just take it easy, Ann..."

Before Miguel could finish, a loud bang came from below us. Before realizing it was actually just Nick's shop opening up, the room had faded into Josh's lab and I watched Matt die again.

"Matt!" I screamed out.

"Annie, it's okay," he said as he hit the ground. "It was only the garage downstairs."

"What?" I asked, confused.

"The guys were just starting up some of the machines at the shop." Miguel was sitting in front of me. I was back in Nick's apartment and Matt was gone. I clasped my hand over my mouth and shut my eyes tight. *What's going on?*

"I'm gonna..." I pointed to the bed.

"You didn't hurt anyone," Emily consoled, reaching for me.

"No!" I screamed, then calmed myself. "No ... umm. I'm gonna lay down."

I closed the door to the bedroom and buried myself under the blankets. But I couldn't sleep at first. Not a wink. The piercing pain in my heart made sure of that.

Instead, I tried to cover the sight of Matt's death with the memories of our journeys.

But all I kept hearing was the gunshot echoing through my mind.

A few hours later Emily came to wake me. My dreams had been plagued with Matt.

"Hey." She tapped my shoulder softly, sitting on the edge of the bed. "Joseph just flew in. We are going to meet him at the police station. Do you want to come?"

I shook my head.

"Okay, I'll just send the guys and stay here with you." She walked to the door, then looked back. "Do you want anything to eat?"

I shook my head again.

She smiled briefly, then left.

I didn't want food. Quite honestly, I didn't want to do anything at all. Just lie here and let the world fuck off.

21

TRAPPED

The day of the wake came and I finally got myself out of bed. Emily took the liberty of getting me a dress. I took my time blowing my hair out, making sure it looked perfect for him.

We drove in silence to the funeral home. When we pulled into the parking lot I did not want to get out of the car. All my energy, all of my drive was gone. Nick walked around to the passenger side and helped me out. We walked toward the doors, his hand in mine; I leaned into him for support.

There was next to no one there. It was me, Emily, Miguel and Nick. Matt's brother, Joseph, had brought a handful of his army friends, each dressed in their crisp dress uniforms, plus a few stragglers who just wanted to give their respects. In Matt's defense, we didn't spend much time in the town.

"You must be Annie," Joseph said. "Matt wrote to me constantly about you. The pictures do not do you justice.

May I?" He opened his arms wide. I stepped forward and let him embrace me. My head only reached his chest. His height dwarfed me and I was even wearing heels.

"I'm sorry," I mumbled into his shirt.

"Don't apologize. I never saw Matt love *anything* as much as he loved you," he said, pulling away. "As you and I both know, he would not want you blaming yourself." He held his arm out, "Walk with me?" His kindness was overwhelming when the inside of me was filled with anger. Tears welled up in my eyes and I nodded.

We walked the rest of the short distance in silence, the casket coming into view. As my knees weakened I felt Joseph's arm tighten. I looked up at him with a silent thank you.

I could finally see Matt in the open casket. His face had been cleaned of the blood and he wore a navy-blue suit that perfectly matched my dress. This time my knees collapsed beneath me and I landed on the step in front of the casket. The tears could no longer be held back.

I prayed for the first time in my life that day.

"Dear Lord," I mouthed inaudibly. "I guess you already know I don't pray. Sorry about that. I mean, you haven't given me the nicest hand of cards, if you know what I mean. Anyway, I'll only ask this one thing. Let him live like the angels. He deserves a first-class seat up there. Please ..." I turned my eyes skyward. "I'll miss you always, Matthew Lance."

We all sat and Joseph stepped up to the podium.

"Thank you to those who came today. Matt would have been happy to know the people he held most dear were able to mourn together." He glanced at me, then back at his notes. "I'm not a writer, that was his job. I can tell stories though. Matt was quite the adventurer. From the very first step he took, he would explore and examine everything. Not excluding climbing trees at six years old or sticking beads up his nose, ending us up in the emergency room." He chuckled. "Fearless. He was truly fearless. So, when he got his abilities it wasn't surprising that it would involve travel. I'm sure you guys remember him traveling to our base just because I told him I forgot flip flops for the showers. He just showed up! We were all so damn surprised but for him, it was just another day." Joseph's friends laughed. "He ... he was a light that shone—brighter than most. He was loved. There aren't many people like him in this world. We were lucky to have spent the time we had with him." A tear streaked its way down his face. "It's not fair that he was taken this early. It's easy to let anger consume us. But try, on his behalf, to remember only the good. Thanks."

After that I couldn't hear anything else. It all went by in a blur. Then finally the soldiers with Joseph began to carry the casket out of the funeral home.

Outside, however, a small group of people had gathered holding signs and shouting at the casket.

The signs carried awful anti-Power remarks. I can't remember the exact phrases but man was I livid. Then a woman shouted, "Good riddance!"

Before anyone even had time to react, I was closing the distance between her and myself. My eyes turned a bright blue with power, anger taking me over. I grabbed her by her jacket and pulled her close to my face.

"See, it almost sounded like you were insulting the man I love, but that couldn't be because that would make you a complete and total moron."

"You Powers are nothing but dangerous! See!"

"Annie!" Everyone was shouting for my attention and

running toward me —including the cops stationed at the funeral. But I was too far gone in my anger to hear them.

"You stupid, crazy bitch. You don't know *me*, you don't know *him*," I said, gesturing to the hearse. I felt hands grabbing me, pulling me back. The three cops stepped between me and the lady while Nick, Joseph, Miguel, and one of the army guys struggled to pull me away. Then one of the cops raised his gun.

"That's not necessary, officer!" Joseph yelled, stepping forward. "It was a misunderstanding."

"I misunderstood *nothing*," I screamed.

"Annie, shut up," Nick said quietly. "You need to breathe." Oh I was breathing alright.

"Step aside," the cop directed the men trying to hold me back. They hesitated momentarily but then each obeyed, leaving me standing alone in front of the barrel of the gun.

"That gun is pointless, *officer*."

"Put your hands behind your head, girl." I slowly did what he commanded, finally calming myself. The lady watched me with a satisfied grin while her friends gathered around her to talk of her bravery.

So being the stupid-ass Power that I am, as I lifted my hands behind my head, I activated my powers allowing the strands of light to hover harmlessly around my hands. The cops, however, thought I was going to attack. They grabbed their batons and began beating me, continuing until I remained still. They dragged me into the back of a police car and began driving.

They brought me to a place across town I had never been before. The police car was let through a gate leading to a small building. I was violently dragged out of the car and led into the building, guns trained on my head. I remained silent as they checked me in at the front desk. A buzzer sounded and the officers pushed me through. We walked down a bleak hallway lit by the most terrible LED lights imaginable. We passed a room full of computers and walked down a set of stairs ending in another gate that we were buzzed passed. They strapped me to a bed in a completely white room. I squinted as my eyes tried to adjust to the unnecessary brightness of the lights and I looked around.

There was one long window high on one of the walls, which I figured was the view from the computer room. There were large holes in the ceiling I assumed were there to release some sort of gas. In the corner was a toilet and a shower head with a drain beneath it. Some sort of solitary confinement. *Great.*

Shortly after the cops left, the door opened again and in walked our fair town's police chief, Victor Lawrence. This man practically single-handedly sustained Josh's alliance with the police. He was yet another reason Josh could get away with so much shit—not the whole reason though, seeing as Josh was the reason the Triad was stopped. The police just didn't care about Powers. At all.

I just stared at him. "Do you like the room? Mr. Hunter built it. One hundred percent Power proof," he said, tapping the wall approvingly. I think he was expecting a reaction but I was in no mood to give a crap. Actually, I wasn't in any mood at all—I was empty. The flashbacks of Matt were the only things that told me I was still alive.

"The silent treatment, huh? That's fine," he said. "The doctor will be here tomorrow to diagnose and medicate you. *I* don't particularly care about what is wrong with you, but I'd like to stop any future violent outbursts."

"Do you ever shut up?" I interjected. He walked over to me menacingly.

"Excuse me?"

"Do. You. Ever. Shut. Up?" I asked, dragging each word out for emphasis.

He took a deep breath and began unstrapping me from the bed, "Well, we will be watching you. We do have power restraints, but you'll decide whether we need to use them or not. Sound good?" He left and the sound of the door slamming behind him triggered a flashback of Matt's death.

I rolled onto my side and pulled the covers up. *I can't handle this.* It's bad enough I dealt with it once. I pushed it back, ignored it. Or at least tried. As I did that, I became more and more isolated within myself.

❈ ❈ ❈

I can only imagine the absolute excitement watching me lying around all day must have produced for these guards, but I didn't care and honestly I don't remember much.

However, I do remember two men approaching my bed that night. The room filling with gas, numbing my movements. They stared at me, smiling as they started removing their pants. For the next hour or two these animals took control. I couldn't move, I couldn't speak, and I couldn't fight. I was numb to the world. I became even more withdrawn.

When they finally left, the only thing moving was my tears. I curled into a ball when I got motion back wondering what I had done to deserve this. It was then I felt something for the first time in a while. Hopeless. Fearful. I got up and screamed at the walls. I started shooting at everything with my powers. I fell to my knees and held my face in my hands.

"Fuck!"

* * *

It took me what felt like hours to fall asleep that night. I woke up to the sound of the door opening and watched as a tiny, squirrely man made his way toward me. He had scraggly hair and big, last-century glasses. "Hello." His voice was nasal. He was like a little timid mouse. *And they sent him in here?* Then two other men came in, assumedly to help him.

"I am Doctor Volk and this here is Sebastian and Peter. We are here to help you." I wasn't even looking at them anymore.

Help me? Bring my boyfriend back. That will help me.

"Annie, can you hear me?"

cricket cricket

Matt, I miss you.... I miss you so much. I need to get out of this place. How? I thought.

"Annie, I need to ask you some questions." *What kind of friggin' questions could he possibly ask? Why did you lose your shit and end up here? Hey, how was it watching your boyfriend killed in front of you? How did that feel? Do you enjoy being raped at night? Fuck him. Fuck all of them.* I wasn't moving a muscle.

"I am here to find out when you can be released, so your cooperation will speed things along." I spit at his feet. "Okay, let's begin." He put his briefcase on his lap then asked for a table to be brought in. I jumped when the door opened one minute later and a guard carried in a small table, on which the doctor set his briefcase. Then the door slammed shut. Another flashback of the gunshot I couldn't push back; I sat straight up screaming.

"Matt!!! NO! Please!" I reached my hand out. "Stop! Josh! No!" The two men came and pushed me back down.

As I struggled against them the doctor injected me with something.

"Annie, you must be calm. Tell me what you saw."

"Fuck you! He killed him!"

"Who killed who?"

"Josh! You rat-nosed moron. Josh killed Matt!"

I shook the two men loose and sprung out of bed. Grabbing the doctor by his stupid white lab coat, I pushed him against the wall. "I watched him die. No one is safe from Josh Hunter. Get me out of here!"

"Calm down. Everything will be alright," he said, trying to calm me with platitudes. The two men were trying to pull me off but it was useless; they would have had better luck moving a statue. I lashed out at them and they flew across the room. I heard men running down the stairs to my cell. Five men in black Kevlar with machine guns in their hands entered the room.

"Miss Winters, release him immediately and put your hands behind your head," said the security officer in charge.

"You'll see. Doctor ... " I said, refusing to loosen my grip.

"Now!" The officers raised their guns higher.

"You'll see." I started laughing as I backed up and locked my fingers behind my head. "You will *all* see."

22

NICK

"I have been waiting two weeks! Two weeks and no answer from you people. I have the right to see her."

"Let me get the chief," responded the *highly* uninterested receptionist.

"Jeez. Hopefully we'll get somewhere," I retorted.

I had called the department three times—probably more—every day since they took Annie and they shrugged me off each time. They were keeping her in a facility separate from the police department itself, or so they said, but I couldn't find it for the life of me.

"Mr. Winters, good evening," Chief Lawrence said, walking forward.

"Nick is fine. Bring me to her," I said impatiently.

"I will get a patrol car and take you to her. I apologize for the wait. She should be stable enough for visitors now," the chief continued.

"Stable enough?" I rolled my eyes. "Okay. Whatever you say." I followed him to a squad car and he motioned for me to get in.

"I can drive myself," I said, motioning to my car in the parking lot.

"Of course," the chief said with attitude.

I followed the chief to a facility that was about twenty minutes away and when we got there I couldn't believe I had never seen it before despite the heavy forest hiding it. The building was enclosed by a large chain-link fence topped by barbed wire. The building itself was a windowless, one-level, brick, prison-looking shit zone. I parked and was guided to the door as the chief swiped in. We walked down a windowless hallway with a dank feeling to it, then finally reached the gate. He showed his ID and the gate slid open as a buzzer sounded. I looked at the gate with disgust. *What do they need that for?*

We entered a room that did not fit in with the rest of the building. It was filled with high-end computers and surveillance equipment placed in front of a window looking into a blank white room.

"What the hell? Is that where she is?" I ran up to the window. "Annie!" I turned to the guards. "Let me in there."

The chief nodded his head and a guard walked me down the stairs to yet another gate. Another buzzer let us through and then he swiped a card to let me into the room. *Jeez, what do they think she is going to do?*

"Annie." She was sitting in a corner, curled in a ball. She was still wearing the dress from the funeral. I had never seen her in such bad shape. She looked like she hadn't showered or slept in days. She finally looked at me. There was no life in her eyes.

"Nick?" Barely even a whisper.

She was balled into the corner of the bare room. When I placed my hand on her knee, she jumped. "It's me, Annie, it's me." I put my hands in the air, showing her I was not a threat. Her eyes lightened and she crawled to me. I wrapped my arms around her, hoping to make her feel even a little safer. "I'm sorry it took me so long to see you."

"Please get me out of here, Nick. Please," she said dejectedly. I felt sick.

"I can't." I felt terrible saying that. "I'm sorry." She started crying. "What are they doing to you, Annie? What's wrong?" But she backed away.

"Nothing, they aren't doing anything. I just don't like it here," she said abruptly.

"Are you sure?" She was clearly avoiding something.

"Yes," she said, not meeting my eyes.

"Okay," I surrendered. "Well come back over here. Let me sit with you." We sat on the bed and I put my arm around her. She just stared into space. "You look hungry, Ann. Have you eaten?" She shook her head. "Have you showered?" She shook again. "Do you speak?" She looked down. "Listen, I don't know what they are doing to you, but you can't let them destroy you." It was hard seeing her like this. "I brought you some clothes." I patted the folded outfit on the bed. Her favorite things. A comfy pair of jeans and a T-shirt.

"Thank you for coming to see me," she said robotically.

"Come on, sis. Talk to me. Please."

"I'm leaving soon," her eyes snapped to mine.

"What?" I could see the wheels turning in her head.

"I'm getting out of here. If I don't see you, I love you. Tell Emily and Miguel I love them too."

"You can't just *walk* out of here. Trust me. They have a little bit too much security. What are you going to do?" She became silent again. The door opened.

"It's time to go," an officer announced.

"Okay, hold on." I looked back at her. "Annie, please answer me." She smiled and looked up at me.

"Sir?" prompted the officer.

"Okay, okay," I said to the officer, not taking my eyes off of Annie. "I'll be back tomorrow," I promised before kissing her on the forehead and leaving.

23
NOT STAYING

When I was sitting with Nick I knew exactly what I had to do. There was really only one way to get out of this place. I had to take my necklace off. I didn't want to, but at the time it seemed like the only option. Of course, I had another guest on his way in later that same day—a much less desired one at that.

"Hello, my dear Miss James."

"What are *you* doing here?" I said through clenched teeth.

"What? Is there something stating that I am not permitted to visit?" I just glared at him.

"Get away from me."

"I am sorry, Annie." I jumped out at him, but he held me down with his powers. He walked over to the bed shaking his head. "Tsk tsk tsk."

"You aren't sorry, you piece of shit," I said, seething. "I

won't move. Just let go." He tilted his head, giving me a doubtful glance. "I won't," I repeated. He released his hold and sat on the bed. I can tell you right now, it took a lot of restraint not to punch him in his arrogant face.

"Perhaps if you behave I will tell them to give you respite from your nightly activities," he smirked.

The fact that he could be behind that both did and did not surprise me. My breathing got heavier. I was so unbearably angry, I almost started tearing up from keeping the anger at bay. I got off the bed and walked to the corner of the room.

"Get the *fuck* away from me *right* now."

"No need to be rude, Miss James. No need."

"You killed my boyfriend! In front of me! I have a pressing *need* to be rude!"

He lunged at me, slamming his arms into the wall on either side of my head. I nearly jumped out of my skin.

His eyes were glowing slightly, which made him more menacing. He smiled, "What is it that you thought would happen? Happily ever after? You *belong* to me. You always will."

"Why are you doing this?"

He chuckled. "I need you out of the picture. If you are in here, I can concentrate more directly on the future I have planned for this world, and on killing your kind." I put my head down.

"*Our* kind," I corrected him.

"Enjoy your stay." The truth of my comment had sunk in and he walked out tightening his suit in an agitated manner.

The only reason I didn't chase after him was because I would be making my way out not much later. I listened in as he left and started a conversation with the chief. I didn't have power restraints on, which meant I could hear everything crystal clear, even through the walls.

"I do not believe she is ready to go anywhere yet, Chief." Josh stated.

"I agree. She attacked the doctor and we had to sedate her. I don't know if her nightly punishment is making it any better."

"That is up to me to decide, Victor."

I couldn't wait any more. I reached behind my neck and unclasped my necklace. I watched strands of light flow into me from the stone. I breathed out as my eyes burned and changed to a bright green. I felt her taking over.

"Mea, get me out of here," I whispered.

"Keep her under surveillance, Chief. Do not alter any plans," said Josh, unaware of what had just happened.

"Will do. But what is she doing?"

Josh walked up to the window. I saw him appear and I flashed him a smile.

"Get your men out of here immediately," he said, his voice changing from cocky to downright panicked.

"Why?" the chief pressed.

"Do not question me," Josh snapped.

"With all due respect, Hunter, it is our job to keep her here," said the chief, clearly not understanding what was about to happen.

"You asked me what she is doing. I responded. Your men have no chance."

"No, they won't," I said, allowing my voice to echo through the building.

"Get all the men up here," Lawrence called into the intercom.

"You are making a colossal mistake, Chief. Trust me,"

Josh said, refusing to take his eyes off of me.

As he spoke, the chief fell to the floor. Pushing my voice into his head, I said, "Yes. Yes you are."

I could hear men run into the room above. I laughed as my room started to fill with my P.T. Looking at the camera in the corner of my jail cell, I lifted the door out of its place and threw it to the side.

Once I got through, there was only a simple gate between me and my captors. I waved my hand over it and the metal melted into nothingness. I walked up the stairs, my eyes glowing, and looked around. There were control panels and computers monitoring my former prison. *Fools*, I thought.

Guns were pointed at my face and I could hear more men coming down the hall.

"Put your hands down facing away," a man shouted from the group. "Lock them behind your back. Now!"

"You know," I said, grinning as I walked toward them, "you probably should have listened to *Mr. Hunter*."

"Ma'am, we will be forced to shoot," the guard said with a shaky voice.

I laughed. "Go ahead. Give it a try." I looked at the chief as I shot them out of my way with my powers.

"NO!" I suddenly shouted, afraid of who I was becoming. When my necklace comes off the power it normally restrains is released back into me and manifests itself into an entirely different persona. She takes over me. But sometimes I can fight her. I call her Mea. "Mea ... please," I forced out. "I need you to get me out... That's all. Don't ... hurt ... them."

"Shut up, Annie! You let me out; it's my turn now," Mea responded.

"Mea!"

"So where are the assholes who rubbed me the wrong way? Hmm?" I looked ... well, I mean really she ... um, we looked at Chief Lawrence. "Where do they live?"

Josh moved in front of me. "Annie. Give me the necklace." He reached his hand forward and we grabbed his arm with both hands. We swung him around, sending him flying into a wall, which crumbled against the impact.

"Annie, this is crazy! You've got to stop," the chief said, quaking with fear. This pleased Mea.

"I don't have time to listen to you beg, as much as I would enjoy it," we picked him up and threw him against the wall, too. "Let's find these fuckers," Mea said, putting our hand on the computer.

"Mea." I got through to her again. "We don't need to get them. Let it go."

"Let it go? They did it to me too, Annie. We are the same; don't forget." I watched as she searched through the database, the pages of info flashing through our mind, and she found the addresses of the two men who had raped us.

"No," I said, struggling to get the words out and regain control. "We are ver... different."

"GO AWAY, ANNIE!" She pushed me so far into myself, I could only watch her moving my body around.

"Get your men out, Chief," Josh ordered as he pushed himself out of the rubble. "Miss James!"

"Oh Joshy boy. Annie isn't here."

"Annie," he gasped out as Mea lifted him in the air with our powers and held him still.

"I feel what she feels. You don't want to mess with *me* though." Blood began dripping from Josh's mouth and nose. Mea threw him across the room but quickly grabbed him and lifted him again, throwing him up and through the ceiling. He went straight through, busting through the roof. Then we started to rise. Mea's powers were limitless.

We flew out of the hole and looked down. Josh was lying motionless on the ground. "We will finish this another time, Hunter man." We flew away and my battle against her continued.

The house of one of the guards came into view, matching the satellite image from the computer. "There's numba one." She slammed to the ground. "Let's do this shit." Using our mind, the front door flew open and we walked through it. "Yoohoo! Anybody home?" *Stop, Mea.* I said in our head. A little boy came out of one of the rooms and just looked at us.

"How come you broke the door?" he asked innocently.

"I am looking for someone. Your dad. I think," Mea said calmly.

"He's at the gym."

"What gym?" She asked.

He shrugged. "I dunno."

Mea walked up to him. "Okay. Stay still." But he didn't, so she held him there, putting her hand on his head and closing her eyes. She then quickly sifted through his memories. We traveled down roads, around turns until finally, "got it." She shot out the door and before I knew it, we were at the gym. Unluckily for him, he was just leaving.

"Hello there, good sir."

"Woah! Annie. You're, uh ... you're out. Your eyes." He stumbled over his words.

"Sexy? Hmm? Am I turning you on?"

"No.... I uh. How did you get out?" he stuttered.

"Good behavior, obviously." She walked us over to him.

"I just wanted to return the favor you gave me." He backed up until we were standing in the parking garage underneath the gym. "Let me show you how it feels to be touched when you don't want it." With our powers we grabbed his, well, package, which paralyzed him. Our other hand went up and I tried to push it back but I couldn't. She opened our hand and aimed it toward him. I watched as blood dripped from his eyes, nose, and mouth.

"What are you doing to me?" he screamed.

"Crushing your insides." I watched the life leave his eyes and his body fall to the ground. There was nothing I could do. It was done within three seconds. Mea walked us away from this horrible scene, brushing her hands together, clearly pleased with a job well done.

She was flying to the next house while I continued my struggle to get ahold of her. It was almost as if I had to fight through a sort of paralysis, to gain control of my own body and mind once more. Every time I pushed, she pushed right back with stronger conviction. Finally, I reached a point of weakness and went for it. I quickly lost the ability to fly and we fell to the ground with a loud slam.

"Mea, you can't keep doing this. They don't deserve to die."

"What?! You know what they did to us," she argued.

"Yes I do and I am furious but I can't let you kill anyone. That man had a family!"

"Yeah so what was he doing fucking us!? Huh?" As she was fighting me I reached into my pocket, my hand shaking with effort, to grab my necklace. "No you don't." She pulled my arm back. "I'm not going back. You don't have the balls to do what needs to be done. You're a Power, Annie. You realize that?" I pushed harder and harder to get to my pocket. Each inch I moved, she pulled me back two more. "Those men will *never* face trial. You are nothing to them!" She had a momentary flash of rage and I used that opening to grab my necklace and start moving it toward my neck.

"I don't know why I ever take this off."

"You ... need ... me." She was getting weaker as I fought against her pushes and I got the necklace back on. A bright light shone from my eyes and returned to my necklace as I fell to my back. I looked at my hands and sure enough the blood came. Because of the amount of strength Mea had added to me, my body crashed when I returned to my normal self. Blood came out of my hands, as if my skin couldn't hold it in anymore.

I knew that the man she had killed did not deserve a wonderful life, but he sure didn't deserve to die. He deserved to rot eternally in jail. However, she made a good point, they would never face trial. Not in a world where Powers have no rights. *Does that justify death?*

I looked up at the sky wondering what my next move would be. I sure as hell couldn't go back to my house. Surely the police, or at least Josh, would be waiting and my uncle would sell me out in a heartbeat. I had to leave. Leave and disappear. I had heard about a place in California....

Not two seconds later police cars pulled around me, sirens blaring.

"I'm not going back!" I shouted.

The chief stepped out along with Josh. Josh stared at me with his devilish eyes full of triumph.

"Annie, you're a danger to everyone around you," the chief yelled.

"I won't hurt anyone. Back off!" I called in return.

Josh limped forward, his head bleeding. "You killed seven people, Miss James."

I was struck silent. I lowered my hands. "What?"

"You killed seven people when you broke out. You are to be placed in my custody indefinitely."

"No ... no ... I." I started backing away. "You're lying."

"Unfortunately not, my dear." A tear rolled down my face as he stepped toward me and attached my container bracelets to my wrist. *How could I have done such a thing? Also, when?*

"I did not kill seven people!" I insisted as men dragged me into a van.

"I will keep her under twenty-four-hour surveillance. I can assure you she will be dealt with accordingly," Josh told the chief.

"I lost good men because of her. Don't release her unless you deem it necessary," the chief said.

"She will not be released any time soon. I am sorry you and I had to reconnect this way, Victor."

"Why? You are taking a pest off my shoulders. She is your problem now." They laughed and Josh slowly made his way to the van.

"We must meet for lunch soon. Have a brilliant day."

He sat on a bench in the van, watching me closely. "Little does he know that you are always my problem. Are you not, Miss James?" I was breathing heavily. "You were correct actually. When you said I was lying. You were right. You killed one person, I killed the other six."

"I knew it," I said, hatred dripping from each word.

"It was necessary. I have great plans for you. For us!

You went a little too far this time."

"*I* went too far?" I exclaimed.

"Matthew was a casualty I was willing to sacrifice. And now you are in my custody for as long as I deem necessary."

"But *you* killed them, Josh. Not me!"

"Who do you think they will believe? A respected member of the Power-eliminating society? Or a dangerous eighteen-year-old girl? Hmm?" he asked.

It was like a trap within a trap, no way out; I would have stayed in that room if I had known Josh was going to take me. That's sayin' something.

"Where are we going?" I asked.

"It is a surprise. But we have places to be and people to find."

"People to find?" I asked, suddenly suspicious.

"Of course! Did you think you were the only Power joining me on this remarkable journey?" I struggled toward him but couldn't move, shackles keeping me against the wall.

"You bastard." We arrived at his building; I was dragged out of the car and he walked me toward a huge truck waiting in front. "I won't let you do this. I won't."

"It is already happening, Miss James." The door of the truck slid open and I could see his plan. The walls were at least a foot thick and there were restraints lining them. A sixteen-wheeler dedicated to retaining and transferring Powers. *Oh Lord.*

At the end of the truck there were larger restraints—a full body restraint. I knew immediately it was for me. He pushed me into it and metal clamps closed around my arms, stomach and legs. My wrist restraints clicked into a slot and I was trapped.

"A little much don't you think?" I asked.

"After your little performance, no precaution is unsubstantiated." He said, tapping the stone hanging from my neck.

"I wish she had killed you. I should have pushed her to kill you."

"We both know you do not kill, and besides, it is my fate to kill *you*, Annie. Not the contrary."

He closed the door. I was submerged in darkness, yelling with anger.

For three hours.

24
NOT IN KANSAS ANYMORE

He was wrong if he thought I would just stand here quietly. Well, I mean I was strapped there so I guess I had no choice there but at least I could make some noise.

"Josh! I know you can hear me!" I knew he wouldn't let anyone drive the truck without him in it. I was his prize. His little trophy. "Josh!!"

The truck stopped abruptly and as the door slid open the light burned my eyes. His presence burned more.

"You witch! This incessant screaming is absolutely infuriating," he screamed agitatedly.

"Don't you call me a witch." I hated that derogatory name.

"Does that not fit you perfectly? Does that not please you?"

I raised my eyebrow and glanced at him. "There is not a single bone in my body that doesn't fucking hate you."

"How will I ever live on without your perpetual love?" He looked at me, his expression empty, heartless. He then injected me with a tranquilizer. I couldn't see very well but I could feel him dragging me somewhere. I felt the clamps snapping back around but as I blacked out, we began to move.

❖ ❖ ❖

"You're just going to let him take you like this? Annie, you can save them. You can stop this."

I jumped out of my sleep with the sound of Matt's voice echoing in my head.

"Matt!" I was breathing heavily. My head was hanging low and I looked around from under my brow to see a bunch of people staring straight in my direction. There were probably about twelve people in the box with me, and from what I could tell, we were on a moving train. They were all whispering.

"She's up."

"Do you really think she is dangerous?"

"Who is she?"

It was clear that they had been talking about me for a while. "My name is Annie. I'm not dangerous. If you're on my side," I added.

"Why are you locked up differently?"

"I'm the class favorite," I laughed a little. They didn't seem amused. "I pissed off the boss."

"How'd you do that?" a girl asked again. Slowly stepping forward.

"Honestly, I was born." She was full of pity. "I see he already found all of your pressure points. Didn't he?"

"It hurt like a bitch," the guy in the corner said, rubbing his forearm, which was wrapped with a metal cuff, similar to the ones Josh put around my wrists, lasers piercing the pressure points.

"That was nothing," I commented, under my breath. Everyone started to join in conversation.

"It gets worse?"

"Fuck."

"Are you serious?"

"You have no idea who you are stuck with," I cut in. "I don't mean to scare you. Josh is a very powerful, very ruthless man. But I will do everything in my power to get you all out of here."

"Why would you help us if you don't even know us?" asked a young boy, skeptically. He couldn't have been a day over fifteen.

"Oh come on. Help us? What is she going to do? Curse the guy out?" a different guy retorted. He was tall, dark skinned, and incredibly built.

"We don't know anything about her, Darren. Let's be honest okay, which one of you is in the heavy restraints?" a new girl said looking him over. He had taken a blow to his manhood; you could see it in his face.

"I'm Karah. Sorry for my brother. He's a douche."

"Shut up, Karah," he shot back.

"Karah. Darren. Nice to meet you," I said calmly. "I'm sorry you all have to meet me this way. However, I would like to meet everyone." I looked around at them. Each of them stated their names. Only one person didn't tell me their name—a guy who seemed afraid of his own shadow. "And you are?" I asked. "I'm not here to hurt you."

"Zach. I'm Zach."

"Okay. Hey, Zach. I don't know if you heard me before. I am Annie James," I said, now deciding to go by my birth name.

"Hi, Annie." He looked absolutely terrified.

"As dangerous as I look," I said looking at all of the restraints, "I promise I'm not going to hurt you."

He looked at me with nervous eyes. "What's going to happen to us?" He was a shy little guy, long hair and dark brown eyes. If his skin had been any paler, you would have mistaken him for a vampire.

"It's not going to be good. I don't know what he plans on doing to us." Of course, Josh walked in as I was talking.

"Good evening, children! We have some new members," he called jovially. About sixteen more people walked in; they looked drained. One of the girls started to struggle, which was a bad choice on her part. Others tried fighting him, but Josh hit them all down. "You will learn exceedingly quickly that it does not pay to be the hero," he reminded the newcomers as he kept them all in a pain hold.

"Stop!" The metal dug into my arms as I pulled against the restraints. "Stop it!" They all lifted off the ground and were pushed into their respective places, chained to the walls with a flick of Josh's wrist.

"Being a hero is something Miss James here cannot appear to let go of." He started removing me from the wall. I just stared at him loathingly. "This beauty is here to be an example for all of you," he told the others. He punched me hard in the stomach and I doubled over. "Little orphan Annie will be our test subject." I cringed, looking at his sadistic smile.

"Leave them out of my life." I knew he was just trying to strike a chord.

"No, let us invite them in." He started electrocuting everyone in the car. So, of course, I punched him straight across the face. His eyes flashed red and he looked at me. He picked me up and slammed me on the ground. He materialized a knife and pushed it into my stomach. I looked around, some people were still recovering from his attack and some were looking away in horror. I watched light release from his hands as he used the knife as a lighting rod. I was rendered paralyzed.

"The current running through her is four times the strength I used on all of you." My chest was tightening. "You will not be leaving; you will not *try* to leave. If any of you try something like this," he said, pointing at me, "the consequences will be a lot worse than a simple knife to the stomach. Quite honestly, it would be a colossal waste of both mine and your own time." I tried getting up but he rested his foot on the blade handle. He looked down at me. "She is living proof that I will not give up. You leave, and I will hunt you down. Never underestimate my resources." His hand gripped the knife. "Do not attempt anything else," he whispered to me as he pushed the knife deeper. "I will not tolerate it any longer." He left and the chains broke, letting everyone walk around.

Karah and a few other Powers came up to me. "You're kidding," she said, horrified. "You never said he was *the* Josh Hunter."

"Well now you know," I said through clenched teeth. I placed my hand on the knife and, with one big cry, pulled it out.

"Why the hell did you punch him? It just made it worse," Darren questioned.

"It made it worse for *me*, but better for everyone else. That's why."

"Seriously? Man, that guy was right. Hero complex." Darren muttered.

"I'll deal with what I need to. I won't let him kill anyone else.... He killed my parents." Silence hit the room. "And he killed my boyfriend right in front of me." I looked around the room. "Unless it's pain, this man does not care what you feel. You don't understand." No one said a word. I quickly wiped away the tears. Realizing my morbidity was starting to take over. "So, the next step is to find out where he is bringing us."

"Maybe not. Did you not just see what he did to everyone? For fun?" Zach said with a wavering voice.

"Yes, and like I said, it doesn't matter what you do, because he will give it to you either way. You could do what he says, and he'd hurt you. You could kiss the ground he walks on, and he'd hurt you. You can't change it," I told them. "But I would rather get my ass handed to me because I did something he hates rather than doing nothing at all."

I walked up to the door Josh had left through and searched for any crack or opening. *Nothing.*

These people didn't deserve this. Most of them were younger than I was. I focused my vision and saw through the other train cars. It's hard to focus my sight through that many walls though, and I began to feel a stinging in my eyes.

"Fuckin' crap." I rested my head on the door, banging my fist against it with frustration. "Joooooosh!" I called, dragging his name out.

"Don't call him back!" a young girl screamed.

"Seriously. I don't think I could handle another pain hold," Karah piped in.

What was I thinking? *I* might have been used to Josh's tortuous techniques, but they had barely just experienced it. They were scared stiff. To them, Josh was an unfamiliar madman. To me, he was a not-so-caring caretaker.

"I'm sorry." I walked to the back of the car and sat down. "Does anyone have any idea of how long we've been moving."

"Three hours forty-two minutes and thirty-six seconds," Zach said. Everyone just looked at him. My eyebrow went straight up.

"A ... Alright." I muttered.

"And we have stopped six times," he added.

"Thank you very much, Zach." I contemplated. "I think this trip is going to end very soon."

"How could you possibly know that?" someone asked.

"I don't, but the train sounds pretty full."

There were about twenty-nine people in the train car I was in. Two of them were in the corner making out. Probably trying to make the best of the time they had. Zach retreated to a group of similarly quiet kids who were whispering to each other about their options. Then there was one girl who clearly didn't hear me mention my late *boyfriend*, because her eyes never left me. There was longing in her eyes. I am not going to lie, she was beautiful, but I just smiled politely.

Every Power in this car was desperately clinging to any possibility of escape. Hope. *Come on, Annie. Think.*

25

FEAR

"So, seriously, why does this guy have it out for you?" Darren asked me, sitting down next to me.

"I wish I could tell you. All I know is he killed my parents. I lived a while without him bothering me, but for the past few years he has made my life a living nightmare."

"People are sick," Karah responded.

"He isn't *people*. He is a fucked-up man whose life is dedicated to killing." A life I could never understand. "But nevermind me. How did you two get caught up in this?"

"Our parents," Darren spit out.

"Our parents are highly Power-phobic. They gave us away to the Power-hunting agency near us. We have been locked up there for the past two years, but I guess we are harder to kill, so they gave us to this guy," Karah said.

"Who we now know is Josh Hunter. The man who stopped the Triad. We are so dead," Darren's voice was full of anger and resignation.

"First of all, you are not dead. It's not going to happen. And second, I am so sorry your parents did this to you. I don't even know what to say."

"They fucking suck. That's all there is to it."

"People fear what they don't understand."

"Ain't that the truth," Darren agreed, then went silent.

"It's not easy. That's for sure." Karah added. "Knowing your parents are scared of you. Then condemn you to this?" she said, motioning to the train car.

"I'm so sorry." And I meant it. "How old are you two?"

"We both just turned eighteen," Darren said.

"We're twins."

"All we've got too. No family to notify when we die."

"Jesus, Darren, chill out," Karah said.

"I . . . I'm not going to let that happen," I said to Darren before he could continue. "I am going to figure something out. For all of us." I said, looking around the train car. *I just don't know what.*

* * *

A short time later the train stopped for good, as I had thought it would, and we were all brought into a large building. There were cages full of Powers in a lab the size of a baseball field. Hundreds of Powers with no way to fight back.

Josh took my wrist restraints off and put me into a Power-proof glass chamber, as usual. There were six other chambers next to me and a Power in each. Josh started working on screens in front of them, working on Formulas.

"Josh!" He ignored me. "Hey Josh!" Nothing. "Don't ignore me, asshole."

"I am working! What could you possibly require?"

"This is insane," I pleaded.

"This," he gestured to the entire facility, "is my job," he said condescendingly. "And since killing you is taking longer than I had anticipated, I have to have keep myself occupied in some manner. Is that a suitable answer for you, Miss James?"

"You're a prick." He moved in front of my chamber and started electrocuting me. I didn't scream. It pissed him off when I didn't scream, and I liked that. Instead, I fell rigid to the floor. My nerves lighting on fire.

He kept it on a five-minute loop, when it finished he had finished creating the Formula for one of the kids—Zach. I could barely see, let alone get myself off the cold ground.

"Simple. It was an incredibly simple DNA structure you had there, young man."

I was scared for Zach. His chamber filled with gas and he backed into a corner.

"Come on! Please don't!" Zach begged.

"Just think how peaceful the world will be with one less Power to darken the days," Josh replied, joy sparkling in his eyes.

It was hard to watch. The color drained from Zach's already pale face and his eyes grew bright for the last time. Josh dragged him out of the chamber and threw him to the center of the room.

"I formally welcome you all. This marks the first victory with many more to come. You will all fulfill the same fate. Escape is not possible. So please, do not waste my time." He stabbed Zach in the heart and stood reveling in his death for a few seconds before he returned to the computer screens.

I had barely known Zach, but I cried for him.

✼ ✼ ✼

It was terrifying to watch Josh kill. A guard brought

another struggling Power into the now empty chamber. The room was silent and even I didn't know what to say. My mom's words ran through my mind. I had to stay strong.

"Josh," I said with a shaky voice.

"Do not bother, Miss James. There is nothing you can do."

And that's exactly how I felt. Helpless. But I had to do something, I had to! People were yelling insults and demands and he ignored all of them.

I finally pulled myself together enough to talk. "Where are we?"

"This is my new facility."

"Facility? We aren't chemicals to be tested, Josh."

"Oh yes, you are, Annie." His voice was colder than ice. "That is exactly what you are."

I spent the rest of the day watching Josh kill off the Powers I should have been protecting. I never realized how easy it was for him; granted, he hasn't been able to find my Formula for years. At this point he had killed thirteen people. Thirteen people in a day, and he couldn't kill me in around three years. I had to act up, do something. He couldn't hurt me. Much.

But what can I do all locked up? I used the next day to conserve my powers and brainstorm a plausible plan. I think Josh kept my chamber full of some sort of weakening gas; my strength was not at its highest and I couldn't seem to recharge. So clearly, I needed to find a way to get out of the chamber.

He killed more and more each day. I couldn't stand waiting. The walls of the building were lined with dozens of cells holding about thirty Powers each. I could see the restraints on all of them and their faces full of fear and hopelessness. I was their only hope and that was a scary thought.

"One day you will be as strong as Daddy and me, even stronger." My mothers' voice echoed in my head. *"Someday other people — people just like you — will look up to your strength and you will be a kind of hope for them."* It was that day. This was my chance.

"You have to stop now," I said calmly.

"Oh please. What is it that you think you can do?" I placed my hand on my necklace and looked at him. "I will progress faster if that necklace comes off your neck, Miss James."

"Let them go. All of them."

"Do not test me." We stared into each other's eyes with loathing.

"You aren't killing me any quicker by sharing your attention, you know."

"I do not need your Formula right now. They must go first."

"I will find a way to release them. You'll have no chance."

He took a deep breath. "This seems like an opportune moment to test my new product."

"And what is that, Josh? Do tell!" I exclaimed with forged excitement.

"You will see," he said with a smirk, as red smoke slowly surrounded me.

The smoke filled my lungs. The doors to the facility opened and in walked Nick, Emily, and Miguel held by guards. "No!" I ran up against the glass. "Nick! Let them go, assholes! Let them go." I was shooting at the walls without any effect of course. "Josh, why are they here?" He didn't answer. The guard pushed them to their knees.

"What are they doing?" I screamed with panic, looking

back and forth between them and Josh. A single guard stood behind each of the people I loved.

"Ready men?"

"Ready for what?" I asked nervously. "Ready for what?" They raised their guns. "No!" My eyes widened, and I fell to my knees with horror.

"Ready!"

"NO! Not ready. Put the guns down!" I cried.

"Aim!" The guns lifted to their heads.

"Please. God no! Josh, I'll do anything." I was crying the Niagara Falls of tears. "What do you want?"

"Fire!"

26
KARAH

I have never heard anyone scream as loudly as she did. The weird part is, she was screaming as if someone were being killed.

"What are you doing to her?" I yelled to Josh.

"Fear gas, darling."

"Fear gas?" I asked skeptically.

"An incredibly powerful hallucinogen that stimulates your brain into bringing your deepest fears forward."

"Annie! You are okay! Nothing happened!" I yelled, trying to make her understand.

"She cannot hear you," Josh said. "Do not attempt to gain her attention. She is beyond your reach."

Annie was kneeling on the ground with her head in her hands and elbows on her thighs. It wasn't right that such acts of terror could keep happening to a person so seemingly good.

"Josh?" It seemed to be hard for her to talk. "Josh, I

can't breathe." She moved her hands to her throat, gasping for air that she thought she couldn't get. "What are you doing to me?" Josh just watched her, with a sickening smile plastered across his face.

When it seemed like she was about to pass out, the air came back. She gasped and stood up. She looked petrified. It was petrifying to watch as well. Her breathing was heavy and long, but she paused.

"Mom?" Josh's head snapped to complete attention. "Mom, I'm sorry. I ... I tried. I know you told me never to take it off. I had ... no choice."

She was hysterical.

"Please no. Please don't leave again. Mom? Mom!"

27
REALITY BITES

The delusions faded away, and I came back to reality only to see Josh speeding away.

"What the hell?"

"Annie? Are you okay?" Karah asked from across the large room. Everyone was staring at me, obviously.

"Yeah, I think so."

"Look, it wasn't real. It was just fear gas making you imagine things, okay?" Karah said. "What did you see?"

"I watched the people I hold most dear to my heart die. And then I couldn't breathe." I know I can't die, but for some reason not being able to breathe terrifies me. Just because I can't die doesn't mean I can't have death-like fears. Right?

"What about your mom? What was that about?"

I stood in front of hundreds, looking completely defenseless in front of all the Powers I needed to save.

"I, uh..." I didn't have a response for them. It felt as if

my mom had been right in front of me. So disappointed. Then she was killed. Again.

No more questions were asked and a few more days passed as I tried to recover from the resurfaced memory. It just felt so real.

It was on the fifth day that I didn't shut up. I talked Josh's ear off in the hopes of pissing him off as much as Powerly possible. Some of the others started yelling as well, he just picked them next. I decided it was fun fact time!

"Josh, did you know that the first scientist to find the platypus thought it's bill was fake, so he thought it was a joke?" He rolled his eyes. "The very first food eaten by a U.S. astronaut in outer space was applesauce. Like, who woulda thunk?"

He looked at me. "Stop. Just, stop."

"Did you know Saturn has sixty-two moons? Pft! And we only get one!" He rubbed his forehead. "Did you know a flash of lightning can power a light bulb for six months?"

"Annie!"

"Did you know I love Snapple? Love. Did you know that mangoes can get sunburn? The patent for the fire hydrant was destroyed in a fire."

He sighed and held is fingers to the bridge of his nose.

"Oh! Oh! You'll like this one. In 1938, Time Magazine chose Adolf Hitler for man of the year. Maybe you'll be next! You kill a lot of innocent people too!"

"Silence!" He walked up to my chamber. "You are nothing special, Annie. You are just like these inadequate aberrations."

"Yeah?" I raised my eyebrow. "Then kill me."

The chamber door slammed open and I jumped. He grabbed me and threw me to the floor.

"What? Can't handle the truth?" I said as he kicked me repeatedly. "Getting under your skin. Huh?"

"You will die by my hand!"

"If that's true, then what's taking so long?" I choked out.

He put me in a pain hold. My body stiffened with a fiery pain. I pushed myself to look at him, but it was hard to move.

"I know what you are doing. You will not distract me from killing every single one of these things!"

It was then that Josh looked up at all the Powers he had locked up and loosened his hold. I used that opening with no hesitation. I brought all the strength I had saved to my hands and with one big force strike I pushed Josh across the room. My hands were glowing so brightly even I didn't want to look at them. I took out the guards by the main gate and as many others as I could. I centralized the cell locks in my mind and broke them.

"Go!" I screamed. Everyone started running down stairs and out the gate I opened for them. They were cheering me on and while they ran past me I broke off all their restraints. "Help each other out! I can't release all of them." I was holding Josh down and other Powers were fighting guards. Bullets were flying.

"Miss James!" His eyes were blood red. "Let me go immediately."

"You will not kill another Power today." He was pushing against me—really hard. It hurt; I could feel it in my hands. Then Karah ran up to me.

"I'm waiting with you."

"Absolutely not!" I said through the strain of holding

Josh down.

"I'm not leaving. Let me help," she insisted.

"The bullets." One had hit my shoulder, another my leg. "Can you take out the guards?"

"Okay. Got it." And with that, she dispatched the guards quickly and efficiently with her powers.

"Thank you. Now go. Help your brother," I told her.

"He's fine. He is helping everyone get out," she reassured.

It was getting harder to keep Josh down. "You need to be safe."

"You will both suffer unforgiving consequences," Josh said, starting to stand up. There were still hundreds of Powers waiting to get out. I looked at them. They watched me in fear. They won't make it.

"Karah, stand still. I am getting us out of here; every one of them." Something was burning within me. A new strength. A memory of Matt. His smile. Paris. Rome … I closed my eyes and focused on all the Powers within two miles of the building, excluding Josh of course. My eyes flashed white and in the blink of an eye we were all in an empty soccer field and I couldn't hold myself up.

It took a few moments of silence for everyone to realize they were safe. When they did, they all began to cheer, and clap, and hug, and smile. The sound was reward enough for me, meanwhile my hands were sore and my head was pounding.

"Darren!" Karah yelled. Darren came running over and turned me onto my back.

"I'm okay," I said softly. Everyone began crowding around me. "Is everyone okay?"

"Okay? Yeah, they are fine. Annie, you've been shot," Darren pointed out.

I looked down to see a nice bloody gunshot in my side, in addition to the ones in my shoulder and leg.

"Well that would explain the piercing pain."

"How did Josh even get a shot in?" Karah pondered.

"I think it was right before she traveled. I heard a shot," someone piped in.

"Did I save all of them? Are they all here?" I asked, momentarily panicked.

"Yes! You just Traveled with hundreds of Powers. You are our concern right now."

I could feel the bullet beginning to release chemicals into me. The pain was excruciating. "Something is wrong." Everything started to spin.

"We need a Healer. Who is a Healer?" A bunch of people stepped forward. They all placed their hands above the wound and began to heal. I threw up.

"Stop! God stop!" I shrieked. Dammit Josh. "You can't remove it," I said, my eyes stinging with the threat of tears.

"Why?" Darren asked, a hint of aggravation in his voice.

"It's a trigger bullet. The more you work on it the more chemicals it will release. It is also most likely a tracker," I added.

"Where the hell does this guy come up with these things?" someone commented.

"We have to get it out," Darren stated.

"Darren. It hurts too much. Please just get everyone somewhere safe. I'm sorry, but all of you have to leave."

"We aren't going anywhere!" someone shouted.

"We are staying!" another person screamed. They all began to scream and shout with newfound excitement.

"We need to get it out," Darren said seriously. "I'm sorry." He held me down with a few others and the Healers did their part. It only took a few seconds for me to pass out because of the chemical release. The pain was unbearable, and for what I've experienced that was saying something.

28

DARREN

I felt bad holding her down when she had just dealt with all that pain inflicted by the most homicidal man known to Powers.

"Okay, Darren, that was a little harsh," Karah hit my arm.

"We need to help her. She saved us. All of us," I responded, remembering the dick comment I made to her on the train.

"Well now what do we do?"

"First, we have to make sure everyone gets home, Karah. I got a feeling if she wakes up and they aren't safe she might throw up again."

"We already told her we aren't leaving. That still stands," piped in some random pipsqueak of a dude.

"And *you* are?"

"Jake."

"Jake. Ah. You speak for everyone?"

"No, but I'm pretty sure that's everyone's opinion." Everyone I could see began nodding their heads in agreement.

"Whatever, man. I have to help her first." I gently picked Annie up and began walking away; everyone followed. There were about four hundred Powers walking the streets of San Francisco. I laughed.

"We need a place to stay," Jake interjected.

"Thank you, Captain Obvious." Man was he annoying. "Did you have an idea?"

"Well I have money if that helps?" Money appeared in his hands. Best thing about him so far. It took a few hours, but we found a few hotels with enough vacancy for all of us. I put Annie into a bed and Karah changed her clothes. Then we played the waiting game.

29
WAKE UP WAKE UP

"He won't stop there, Annie. He will try to kill them. You have to find Josh. He killed your parents. He killed me, Annie. Find him."

"I know!" I woke up screaming.

Matt would have never spoken to me like that. Josh. *He's in my head again.* "GET OUT!" He was trying to manipulate me and unfortunately it was working.

"Annie, what's wrong?" Darren and Karah came running in and I sat straight up.

"What are you guys doing here?" I said with a hint of frustration lacing my words.

"Everyone is here. They all wanted to stay and make sure you were going to be okay," Karah explained.

"Oh God no. You guys don't understand. He is already on the way," I said pushing myself off the bed. "And why do they all care about me?"

"You saved hundreds! Word is spreading very quickly

about what you have done," Karah exclaimed. "There has never been a Power rescue at this scale. Ever!"

I had no time to think about my newfound fame. "How far are we from where I brought us?"

"I dunno. Maybe five miles. Why?" asked Darren.

"I have to go."

"Annie…"

"Karah. I really don't mean to be rude. I appreciate what you've done here, but you guys have no idea what he will do if he finds everyone here. I need to buy them all time to escape to safety."

"He won't find us. We have a few people shielding this place," Karah argued.

"You both have to trust me. He already knows where we are," I pleaded. "He can find the coordinates of the last place the tracker was active. So he is on his way. I need to go to him so he won't find everyone else again. Please trust me once more. Just help them get out." I gave both of them hugs, and I kissed Darren on the cheek. "You aren't as tough as you pretend to be. I can see right through you." I smiled. "I'll find you guys again someday. Don't worry." I left them looking at me with doubt and concern.

They didn't realize how persistent Josh was. He would take down cities to find a single person. And since that person was me, it didn't look good. *What else could I do though? Let them all die? No. No way.* I began walking the streets of San Francisco, planning my next step.

But there was no way to get out of this one. And yet I couldn't help thinking it was worth it. I mean, I released more than four hundred Powers from the clutches of my own personal devil. That counts for something right?

✾ ✾ ✾

As I walked, I found myself getting more and more nervous. Every time I saw a black SUV I jumped, but it was never him. But I knew he was coming. And plus, I knew he must have arrived in California by now. I know he owns an airplane somewhere. I had known him for long enough to know his strategies. This time though, I didn't see it coming. An RV pulled up next to me and there stood Ian, Josh's head guard.

"Get in, Annie."

I looked at him. "What? No tranqs this time?"

"The boss says we won't need them."

"Great." I voluntarily walked into the RV and the guards went to grab me. "Don't touch me. I am not going anywhere." I looked at them, pushing back my frustration.

"J, I have her," Ian said into his earpiece.

"Do not move," said Josh's muffled and disembodied voice.

The RV stayed still and a door opened a little while later.

"Traveling. That is impetuous even for you, Miss James." Josh looked down at me, loosening his tie. "You should have never done what you did. However, I will spare you a modicum of pain because, after all, you did make it quite painless to locate you. They are close by. Correct?"

"They are long gone by now."

"Oh, I am sure. I know you are trying to protect them. But, darling, you cannot. You are simply not a hero."

"I saved them from *you* didn't I?" I retorted.

"Temporarily. I will find them and kill them, slowly and painfully. I will make them suffer through the death you will suffer through when I kill you."

157

"They did nothing to you!" I screamed in his face.

"You did enough!" he screamed right back. He reached forward and palmed my nose. I heard a crack and I fell back holding it. My eyes began watering.

"Fuck!" I shouted. "You son of a b... Ah!"

"It seems to me that you have lost sight of who it is that is in charge," he said pushing my now broken nose, holding it by the bridge. I screamed out in pain. "Did you hear me?" he asked.

"Yes! Yes!" I screamed.

"Your impertinence has been going on for quite long enough now." His voice was ice cold rage.

"I'm sorry!" I pleaded.

"Who is in charge here? Hmm? Me or you?"

"You are. I am sorry!"

"Pardon me?" he asked, urging me to play his little game.

"You are!"

He let go. "Good girl," he said.

"Why me?" I asked, through emotional exhaustion.

"Excuse me?"

"Out of every Power in the whole damn world, why me?" He just stared at me, like a deer in headlights. "You don't treat anyone else the way you treat me. Ever! There has to be a reason."

"It is my job," he said, pulling his suit taut.

"Oh please," I said, not buying it for a second.

"It is none of your concern."

"Are you kidding me? It is beyond my concern" I snapped.

"Watch your tone, Miss James," he warned.

"Well tell me then! With everything you have done to me, you owe me an explanation. You owe me at least that."

He was breathing deeply. Looking away from me. His eyes wandered, looking anywhere but at me. His jaw clenching.

"Why can't you look at me?" He was acting weirdly. Never, in my many years of Josh experiences, had I seen him nervous.

"I met your mother when I was fifty-five; she was twenty-seven. Of course I did not look fifty-five. I looked probably thirty. I was not as ruthless and jaded as I am now — on the outside at least. She did not know I was a Hunter. I was not as known as my father was. When we met I could not stop staring at her."

My mouth dropped. Him and my mom? No way. No.

"I knew right away that she was a Power. I could sense the power radiating from her. I introduced myself and immediately our emotions for each other grew."

"You are lying."

He shook his head. "We started dating a month later."

"She would never date someone like you," I shouted.

"Oh but she did, Annie. We were so in love. For the first time in my life, I did not feel like I needed to hunt. She took precedence over everything."

"Oh God, oh God. No.... Nope!" I refused to believe it. *Absolutely not.*

"Yes. But I did not get to have her forever. We were together three years when she found out certain truths I was withholding from her."

"Like what?"

"Well, she found out that I was a Power Hunter, that

I had killed over a hundred Powers. Then she found out I had killed my father."

"Wait, you killed your own father?" I questioned, not believing even Josh capable of something like that.

"He was a threat. I had no choice in the matter. He discovered two years into my relationship with your mother that I was not executing my duties as a Hunter. He told me if I did not return to my responsibilities he would kill her. I could not allow that. So one day when your mother was out, I went and took his life. I am still unsure how she discovered this, but she did. She looked at me as if I were a monster. We fought and fought. I told her he would have killed her, but she said there was no excuse. She left. I felt like my heart had been ripped out." He turned away from me and cleared his throat. "I searched for her everywhere. For months and months. I could not figure out what else I was to do."

It was so weird to see him showing actual feelings and emotions.

"I found her five months later. She had been shielding herself from me. She was already dating Trevor James. I was furious. I could not believe she had moved on so quickly. She betrayed me."

"She was clearly afraid of you, Josh," I said, defending my mother.

"I would have never hurt her." I looked up; his eyes had glazed over. "I stayed calm enough to talk when I found her," he seemed to zone out while telling me the story, immersed again.

"Josh, I can't stay with you, sweetheart. I can't trust you," Lisa told a younger Josh.

"You can. You can," Josh pleaded. *"I have not hunted since we*

met. I am changing."

"*I know ... but your father, Josh. How could you possibly do such a thing? How can we have a family together when you kill your own flesh and blood.*"

"*I ... Lisa, please. Just give me one last kiss, a parting kiss. We never got to say goodbye.*"

"*That's not a good idea.*" *She turned away from him.*

"*Please,*" *he begged, gently turning her around.*

"I kissed her and she melted into me," Josh told me, shaking his head. His eyes losing their glaze. "We made love for the last time," he said, coming back to the present.

"Oh dear lord, please stop." *Why did I ask?*

"You wanted a reason, Annie. I am simply telling you the truth. I left her and for the next few months I mourned. Ursula found me in the sixth month and brought me to my new self. The Josh you know now. I searched for your mother. Angry, hurt, and vengeful. Only to find her pregnant."

Oh dear God. Tell me David is not my brother, I thought.

"I could not believe she never told me. Not even a phone call. Nothing. I tortured her, tortured Trevor, and I tried to keep her there long enough to receive what was rightfully mine. But, she escaped. So instead of catching her, I watched, and on May 18, 2035, she went to the hospital to deliver a perfect little girl. I attempted to eliminate this child but apparently, in my *fit* of childish rage, I picked up the wrong one ... " he said with exasperation in his voice.

"Wait stop. I think I am going to be sick," I interjected. That is *my* birthday.

"... because *you* are still here," he continued.

"You're lying." The room was spinning, my stomach a knot with anxiety.

"I am not lying, Annie."

"I am not your daughter. I'm not. It is impossible." *There is no way in any world of worlds that this man, the target of my hatred, is my father,* I thought.

"It is not impossible."

"It is!"

I moved away from him, sitting on the RV's bed. I pushed myself into the corner, just wanting to get out of the damn place. He stood at the end of the bed, calmly. I looked into his eyes and he looked back. He wasn't lying. I could tell.

"Why haven't you told me this before?" I asked, almost whispering. "If you are my father, then why haven't you used your powers to kill me? You're the only one who can. You could have been done with me years ago."

"Do you not think I have tried? Dozens of times. However, I.... Your body somehow built an immunity to my abilities. Something even I did not think a possibility"

"That's insane," I said, running the story through my mind over and over again.

How can I find out for sure? There has to be a way.

A scary concentration rested in his gaze.

I aimed my hand at the engine and stopped the RV. Ian stepped forward but Josh held his hand up and shook his head. I ran out the door and leaned against the vehicle to catch my breath and gather myself.

No wonder he had such a need to kill me. I was the one person, other than David, that could kill Josh. The one person that could make an immortal man fear for his life.

I needed my brother. My one true source of hope. I focused really hard on home, hoping to travel again. *Nick, I need you,* I thought and with that I was home, hoping Nick was here, and not at his apartment.

He popped his head out from the kitchen. "Holy shit," Nick said as he ran to me. "Holy shit, thank God," his strong arms wrapped around me.

I burst into tears. Like ugly cry tears. "You'll never believe what happened. What I just learned. *I* still can't."

"Try me."

I took a giant breath, the words feeling fake, "Josh is my father."

His jaw dropped and for the next hour I explained what had happened since I had broken out of police confinement.

"You are one hundred percent sure?" he asked.

"I think so ... yeah."

"Jeez." He ran his hand through his blonde hair.

"Yeah but, Nick, please don't tell anyone."

"I won't. Don't worry."

"I am exhausted. Emotionally. I mean..." I just sighed.

"Why don't we just relax a little?"

"That sounds great."

"I thought so." He kissed me on the forehead and I rested my head on his chest. I closed my eyes, by choice, for the first time in a while.

30

NICK

So, I stayed with her. For once she could depend on someone to watch over her. As usual, her respite was short. Ten hours later a knock caught my attention. I slipped out of the room to see my dad opening the door to the one and only.

"Hello, Mr. Winters. Is Annie here?" Josh asked.

"Yeah, she is upstairs with Nick. Annie, get your ass down here!" my dad yelled up the stairs. I came down instead.

"What the hell do you think you are doing here?" I yelled, surging toward Josh.

"Annie and I have one final thing to do. So I am picking her up."

"You aren't laying a hand on her, you son of a bitch. You think you can just take her whenever you want?"

"Well yes. Actually," Josh replied calmly.

"You are very wrong," I said through gritted teeth.

"Nicholas, stop it," my dad said.

"Don't tell me to stop," I snapped at my dad, before turning back to Josh. "You think you can come in here and play that card now that it's out on the table. That's not how this works."

"I do not need your permiss..."

"Get away from me." We all turned around and saw Annie standing at the top of the stairs, hands lit up. She was so enraged the light even traveled up her arms.

"Annie! Don't even think about it in this house!" my father warned angrily.

"Tell him to leave," she countered.

"Mr. Winters, may I have a word with her?" Josh said, barely remembering Annie and I were there.

"Absolutely," my dad said, making me increasingly ashamed of him.

"Dad, what are you doing?" I pushed him to the side, but he pushed back pinning me against the wall as Josh ascended the stairs toward Annie.

"He has legal custody over her, Nicholas. The police handed her over when she escaped. I am not getting in trouble over that little piece of shit."

I looked up the stairs as Josh closed the door to Annie's room behind him. *Oh jeez, what is he going to do to her?*

31
GIVE ME A BREAK

"I am not going back with you, Josh. I'm not."

"Yes, you are," he said, but telepathically. "Do you know why I can speak to you this way?"

"I was hoping you were a telepath, but I have growing feeling that that isn't it."

Fun fact. The only Powers who can speak telepathically are Telepaths ... and family. Blood family. Undeniable, genetically related family. Which only means one thing.

"You are correct in believing that," he said, again in my head.

"Telepaths can't talk over a large distance. Only familial ties allow that," I said out loud. More to myself than him. "That's why I heard you that day in school."

He nodded. "It is time to go," he said out loud.

"This is insane."

"I realize it is a lot to process, but quite honestly we

have wasted enough time already. It is time to attend to the next order of business. Do not make me drag you out of here, Miss James."

I looked at him defiantly, shaking my head in disbelief as he grabbed me by the base of my neck and brought me downstairs.

"Hell no! You aren't taking her!" Nick yelled, rushing forward.

"Nick, it's okay. I will be back soon," I told him, not wanting my brother to get hurt. After a pause he stood aside. Stubborn anger splashed across his face. Little did either of us know what I was walking into.

32
DEATH BECOMES HER

"Why am I sitting in the front seat?" I asked, surprised my this turn of events.

"Pardon me?" Josh asked.

"You never drive and I never sit in the front seat of your car. Why am I now?"

"If you would prefer, I will chain you to the seat in the back."

"No. No, I was just asking. You don't treat me like this, ever. What's going on?"

"Let it go, Annie," he said through clenched teeth.

"Fine." But somewhere I knew what was going on in his head. And I knew this calm was deceiving. A few silent minutes passed and we arrived at his lab. He let me walk in. Next to him. It was strange to say the least.

His lab was nearly empty, with nothing but a chair sitting in the center of the room and a small amount of guards stationed around the room. "Please sit," he said, motioning to the chair. "I did not consider that your necklace could possibly affect your genetic makeup. I was wrong." he pulled a syringe from a case a guard was holding open for him. I sat straight up, but two guards stood to my left and right ensuring I would stay put. Not that I couldn't fight them off, but I knew this was the end of the line for me.

I shook my head with a quivering lip. He walked up behind the chair wrapping his arm around my shoulders to hold me still. "Just keep breathing, my love."

"Josh ... please," I begged desperately.

As soon as the needle hit my skin I knew it would be an experience like none other. The pinhead amount on the tip of the needle sent shooting pain through my head. When the serum was injected the pain took over. It felt like lava was coursing slowly through each and every vein in my body. It was attacking everything that made me. My powers were being ripped away. I couldn't stop it.

I shot out of my seat as light shot from my hands and I fell to the ground with writhing pain. It was excruciating and it only got worse. My eyes became blurry with blood. The light continued to shoot from my hands and my fingertips began to bleed. I cried out to Josh but he just stood over me, watching. I felt my strength being drained and I couldn't hold myself up.

I wanted to cry but my eyes were full. I wanted to scream but I couldn't breathe.

My powers shut down for the last time, leaving me lying in a pool of my own blood. I tried to turn over, but failed. Josh started talking to me but I heard nothing over the ringing in my ears. I felt him pick me up and then felt nothing.

The nightmare continuing.

33

NICK

Five minutes after Josh took Annie, my dad left too. Another business trip as if nothing had happened. So when the door opened an hour later, I had no idea what to expect. And jeez, I wish it had been my dad.

In walked Josh, my sister dangling from his arms.

"What did you do?!" He ignored me and walked up the stairs to her room. He placed her into bed so gently I would have thought it was someone else. Then he turned around and gazed into my eyes.

"Your sister will need you when she awakes." He had a very subtle smile that worried me to a whole new level.

"Josh?" I followed him, trying to get him to talk, but he said nothing. He closed the front door and I leaned against it, hitting it with frustration.

After I heard his car pull away I ran upstairs to see if Annie had woken but she was supine and still as stone. "Annie," I said softly, "Annie baby." She was sweating; she never sweats. So I felt her forehead and took her temperature. 104.5! I called Miguel hoping he would be able to bring me some emergency supplies from his father's medical practice. "Miguel, you need to come over. Annie has a 104-degree fever."

"What? How?" I swallowed several times, but I couldn't respond and the line went quiet; both of us had realized there was only one way for this to happen. "I'll be right over," he said, seriousness taking over.

"We are going to take care of you, Ann. I promise," I told her as I sat by her bed with a cool towel on her forehead. A short time later I heard the front door creak open, but before I could panic I heard Miguel's voice.

"Nick?" I heard from downstairs.

"Coming!" Behind Miguel stood Emily, eyes bloodshot—she looked terrible. "Are you okay?" I asked her, sensing that something more had happened.

"Em, why don't you go sit with Annie. We will be right up," Miguel said.

"What's wrong with Emily?" I asked, having never seen her looking so ill.

"There's a video online ... of Annie. It already has thousands of views."

"A video of what?" I asked, a knot forming in my stomach.

"I'm guessing one of the guards took it. It's bad, Nick." Miguel brought it up on YouTube; I was surprised it was even allowed on there. The amount of agony she was in was unbelievable. I couldn't even finish watching it.

"Fuck." I looked away.

"I think it's safe to say her powers are gone."

"Poor Ann," I muttered.

"You saw it?" Emily asked when we walked into Annie's room.

"Yeah," I said, shaking my head. Tears welled in her eyes.

"She doesn't look good, Nick," she said, gulping down more sobs. "What do we do now?"

"I think the best thing we can do is be here for her when she wakes up. I have a feeling she is going to be scared. Very, scared," I said.

"What do we even say to her?" she asked.

"I have no idea," I said, sitting next to Annie. I had no idea I would be watching her fight for her life for four days before she finally woke up.

34
WEAKNESS IS A STRENGTH

I woke up in my bed with Nick, Emily, and Miguel sitting around it.

"Annie!" Nick jumped out of his seat as I groaned to sit up. He hugged me so hard, it hurt. I started to cough so he let go.

"What are you guys doing here? How did I even get here?"

"Josh brought you. We know what happened, Ann. We saw," Nick said.

"You saw? Wh... what do you mean you saw?"

"There is a ... video," Miguel said with his head down. I gasped, horrified that the people I care for the most had seen me at my absolute weakest moment.

"I'm so sorry you guys had to s..."

"There is no reason for you to apologize. At all," Miguel said.

"We are here for you now. You don't have to defend us anymore. You're only human. Now more than ever," Nick added.

I fell into Nick's arms, pressed my face against his chest and began to cry. Everyone came and sat around me, holding me close, comforting me.

I sat thinking for a moment. "Guys. You have to do something for me."

"Anything," they said in a chorus.

"Leave," I said seriously.

"What?" asked Nick, just as Emily said "no" and Miguel said "no way."

"You have to." It was at that moment that I fell back onto my bed. The room was spinning. "Guys, I am so dizzy, I think I'm gonna..." I got up and ran to the bathroom, making the toilet my new home.

"What do we do, Nick?" I heard Emily ask.

"Yeah, we can't leave," Miguel added.

"You ... have to," I said between heaving breaths. I couldn't push myself to my feet, reminding me of when my mother went through this exact same experience. But still she remained so strong through it. "Nick?" I said reluctantly. "I can't get up." I was so embarrassed. Nick and Miguel came and lifted me up to my feet and walked me to my bed. My legs had no strength at all. "I don't think you guys understand how much time Josh spent trying to find my Formula. His life revolved around me and now that I am almost out of the picture his true colors will become even more apparent. I have a feeling human laws will no longer restrict him."

"We aren't leaving." Nick stood firm.

❖ ❖ ❖

A painful cough erupted in my chest, drawing blood. Emily and Miguel had gone downstairs to make dinner, while Nick stayed with me.

"Nick?"

"Yes, Ann?"

"I don't want to die." I looked up at him. He sat on the bed, holding me close.

"I know, Ann, I know. I wish I could change this, trust me."

"I'm not ready. I am not as fearless as I seem. There is so much that I could have done. For myself, for the world. I don't want to die. I'm so scared. This sickness, I have never felt like this before. Even with everything he has put me through. I don't know how my mom did it."

I could tell he didn't really know what to say. It wasn't really the easiest topic of conversation.

"Your mom was a very strong person, but so are you. As weird as it sounds, maybe you'll see them again. You parents. Maybe even Matt." My heart fluttered at the thought of seeing him again.

I sat crying into his chest for a while longer. There were no more words to speak.

Every day that passed was harder than the one before. Even lying in bed, I could feel my strength dwindling and my fears rising. I quickly came down with pneumonia. My dreams became nightmares. I woke up drenched in sweat through the nights. I was becoming increasingly scared. Why wouldn't I be scared though? With me gone Josh could do whatever he wanted. Kill whomever he wanted. I was truly helpless.

35
NIGHTMARE ON ANNIE STREET

It started like any other crappy day of the past week but took a very different turn.

I was lying in bed, per usual, when pain shot through my head. My skull vibrating, with his voice.

"It is time." I slammed my palms into my temples, hoping to ease the pain.

"Get out of my head!" I screamed.

Nick came running in. "Annie?"

"You either come to me, or I come to you and kill them."

"What happened? What's wrong?" Nick asked.

"It is time for me to go," I stated. I pushed myself up slowly, but fell back down. He came to help but I held my hand out. "I got this."

"You can't go there."

"Why? We both know it's going to happen sooner or later. I will not let him take you all down with me."

"Josh won't hurt us. We are human." I pushed past him and began slowly walking down the stairs. "I'm going in with you," Nick said, grabbing his car keys.

"Absolutely not. Drive me there, but you can't come in with me."

"What's going on?" Emily and Miguel had heard the commotion.

"It is time for you to all get far away from here. Don't stop for anything. Not for clothes, not for money, nothing."

"But, An..."

"Nick." I looked him in the eyes as seriously as I could. He nodded reluctantly.

The car ride to Josh's place was silent. All of us unable to think of a single word to utter. Slower than I had thought possible Nick pulled up in front of Josh's building. We got out of the car and I hugged them all for what felt like forever, yet it was still not long enough.

"There is no one in this world who could have been better to me than you all were. Thank you." I turned to the building. "Now leave," a dead calm taking over my voice.

They reluctantly got into the car.

Josh was standing in front of me as soon as I walked into the building.

"Do not touch them, Josh."

"No one gets dying wishes anymore."

I took a big heavy breath in and heard a voice dearer to me than any other.

"Annie!" Nick screamed.

"Nick ...no!" At that moment I felt the cold blade of Josh's knife sink into my chest and I gasped for air. I fell down slowly into Josh's arms and looked up at him, watching a tear fall down his face. He pulled the knife out. Blood sprayed from my mouth as the knife left my heart. I turned my head to look at Nick and reached out to him for the last time. Then I was…

36
GONE

Was this what she felt when Matt was killed right in front of her? I wondered, as I watch Annie, my little sister, die before me.

"No! Annie!" I ran to her picking her up, holding her. "Oh God, oh God." I cried over her body for at least ten minutes before Josh interrupted. He was standing there enjoying this whole thing, by the way.

"Take her to the room, gentlemen," he told his guards.

"No! Don't touch her! Josh, she deserves more than this. Let her have a proper burial."

"Oh no that will not be possible, Mr. Winters. There is much work to do and that will simply get in the way. Which is something she cannot do any longer," he said with a smirk on his face.

"You are a fucking psychopath," I said, rage coursing through me.

"Please. I feel great joy!" He smiled, before turning around and walking away. His men pulled me from her and carried her away. I was in disbelief. *Could this be real?*

They threw Emily, Miguel, and me into a small room and we all just sat there crying in silence for a while.

"What do you think he will do to us?" Emily finally asked. I turned my head toward her slowly, knocking myself out of a daze.

"I . . . I don't know. I don't even understand why we are here. The police will have to intervene."

"He'll probably keep us here until we die. I feel like that is his thing," Miguel suggested.

"This is unreal," Emily said dejectedly.

"Tell me about it." I let myself daze out again. I had no desire to deal with these past events. Not one bit.

37

BLUR

Days, weeks, and months passed in a blur. I could barely remember anything but the screams. There was constant screaming coming from outside the door. There was no way for us to know what was happening. We could only imagine. Which in a way was worse.

We were always hungry. Food made its way through the door maybe once every day, but it was barely enough to feed one of us let alone all three. We were all weak and tired. I hadn't slept much and I tried to stay awake in case anyone came to bother us. They never did. We hadn't thought much about escape. We honestly didn't want to know what was going on outside of our cage. The room was virtually impenetrable.

"I miss her today," I said. They nodded. "Maybe we should try to get out. Annie would never give up."

"Nick, even if we had a plan, he keeps us too weak to

do anything," Miguel said. I ran my hands through my hair, which was long and greasy now.

"It's been three months though. We ... we have to do something," I said dispiritedly.

"Like what?" Emily asked.

"I have no idea." I walked to the door and started banging. "Josh!" I screamed. "Maybe if I do this long enough he will open up. At least we will get some air in here."

After a very sore throat and three days, he opened the door. More like slammed it open, but who cares. My eyes burned from the sudden light.

"Will you stop this incessant yelling?" Josh snapped.

"Why are we still here?" I asked, holding my arm up to block the light.

"Nicholas, I do not need a reason to keep you here. Annie is gone; there is nothing anyone can do. You all belong to me now."

"You are a son of a bitch. We are tired and hungry. What is the point of this?" I asked.

He took a deep breath in, as if I were really taking up so much of his precious time.

"Come with me, Nicholas." I followed him between two guards. We walked into yet another room where he nodded at guards who grabbed me and chained me up in the middle of the room.

"I must admit, I am not as experienced in human torture but for you I will make an exception." They handed him a whip and I yelled as the first crack landed across my back. "Defying my rules is unacceptable, Mr. Winters." Another crack. The pain rippled through my body. I had never felt anything like it. *Crack!*

"Stop!" I begged. *Crack! Crack!*

"I hope you have reviewed your choices." He handed the whip to the men. "Put him back in the other room. Five lashings every day until I say otherwise."

They threw me on the floor and Miguel and Emily helped me to my bed.

"Oh shit." They took what was left of my shirt off of me and used it as bandages. I barely slept that night. The ache was so profound.

What were you thinking? Idiot.

38

EMILY

His back was torn to shreds, and Josh never missed a day. Never ever forgot. Nick started to remain silent. He wouldn't talk to us. The only time we would hear his voice is when he woke up screaming Annie's name. I wished so hard that she would just come crashing through that door, but it never happened.

Josh started letting us take showers once a week. Those days were the best days ever. Like ever ever, but Nick wouldn't move. And if I were him, I don't know if I would want water running over my back either.

We were pretty sure at least two more months had passed, maybe three. It didn't really matter because nothing happened inside our little room and we were clueless to the outside world and the havoc Josh was wreaking. All we ever heard was screaming. It never failed to happen. Different voices screaming out in pain, begging Josh to stop. You could just feel the death crawling up your back.

It was safe to say we were in hell.

39

SLEEPING BEAUTY

An empty room held a single glass coffin. Holding his prized kill. The air was cold and the light showcased her perfect figure. She looked exposed. Her blond hair framed her soft features, which somehow remained full of color. She was truly a "sleeping beauty," despite the dried blood covering her.

It was then that a bright light began to glow. It seemed to come from her neck. A deep humming became louder and louder. Within a few seconds the glass covering her exploded. Shattering into hundreds of pieces that landed around the coffin like a blanket.

The girl shot up from the platform, blue eyes brighter than ever. She looked at her hands in awe and then grabbed the stone draped around her neck. She was alive.

40
No Place Like Home

"…God." My eyes burned, but my body felt amazing. I looked around me, realizing where I was. I was dead. I was in a coffin. I climbed out of it slowly, trying to avoid the shards of glass, but I cut my leg. "Dammit! Thaeeakkyhurt." My words came out a jumbled mess, my mouth dry.

I rolled my eyes but then something happened I couldn't believe. My leg healed. Instantaneously. Normally it took hours to heal wounds without thinking about it.

Not anymore.

I made my way toward two big doors. I walked outside and looked around. Empty. No sound. No movement. Other than some papers flying around like tumble weed.

I looked down to reach for one of the fliers and saw Josh's face on it.

New Government. New Laws. New Days Ahead.

"You have to be kiddin' me." I felt the anger boiling.

This anger was different. I felt a whole new kind of strength. My powers were stronger. I could feel them coursing through my veins. I crumbled up the paper and to my surprise it turned to ash.

I didn't know when it was or how I was. All I knew was the power was boiling inside of me like a battle waiting to start.

"I'll be damned before I let you take another day from this world, Josh." I felt it in the air. I can't run away anymore. This. Means. War.

ACKNOWLEDGMENTS

To start, I will thank the first person who ever learned the meaning of Annie: NikkiAnn Bartelloni. Thank you for listening to me that day, years ago, when I told you about my crazy ideas and the characters within me.

To Em Moratti. Your simple question of "Why don't you write a book?" sent me on a journey I never thought I would be on. Without that, this story would have never reached another's eyes, remaining only in my mind. I will be forever grateful. Thank you, for a great many things.

During a time where darkness was threatening to take me over, there was a group of people who listened to the very beginnings of this story. I would write a new chapter every night in a composition notebook and would read them to all of you the next day. Your excitement kept me going. It helped me to believe this was a story worth telling. So for the people who spent that time with me, wherever you are today, thank you.

To my Staples family—especially Jenna, sorry everyone else—thanks for letting me print my story for the first time. The first day I held a physical copy of my book in my hand will never be forgotten.

Yael Katzwer. Man was I lucky to have found you. I mean, you went above and beyond with every edit of this book. There are probably a few words in the dictionary that could explain how awesome you are but I will leave that up to you to find.

Diana K. I will always remember the sessions you let me spend just reading Annie's story to you, and the unconditional love you showed for this part of me.

Nicole H. Let's be honest, who else keeps me sane? What would I do without you? Honestly. Tell me.

John Kreil. Thank you for having my back through many different things. We have been through some shit, but the one thing I knew you understood was my love for Annie and the importance of this book. Love you, brother.

Ellen Carpinelli. Do I even have to explain myself? You know exactly how much you mean to me and Annie. I love you.

Alicia Jaworski, my mismatched puzzle piece. If anyone in this world understands the magnitude of Annie's meaning, it is you. You understand the depth of emotions I have felt and the tears I have cried while writing each word down on paper. There is no one I wanted to share this with more than you. I will love you always.

To my family, I told you I would finish something I started! Thanks for putting up with my crazy dream of writing a book and for believing in me even though I didn't let you read a single page of it. Even up until publication day. There is simply no family more supportive in the entire world.

Last but most certainly not least, to Annie. You, my love, are more real to me than anyone could possibly imagine. Thanks for waiting so long for your story to be told. Hang in there.